"Is that the way the Claibournes close a deal?" he asked.

"I'm sorry? Did you want something in writing?"

"Nothing so formal." Even while she was sending frantic signals to her brain, he raised his hand, sliding his fingers through her hair, cradling her head, holding her captive. He gave her his personal interpretation of sealing an agreement with a kiss.

This was a kiss intended to make a lasting impression. He was completely in control, while she was hot, flushed and vibrantly aware that every cell in her body was being given a wake-up call.

"Now," he said, "we have a deal."

Dear Reader,

Welcome to the climax of my new trilogy, BOARDROOM BRIDEGROOMS.

I do hope you've enjoyed reading about the three talented Claibourne sisters—Romana, Flora and India. I've loved writing their stories, bringing to life the drama and emotion as they've clashed with the Farradays, three dynamic businessmen determined to regain control of Claibourne & Farraday, "the most stylish department store in London."

This time it's India's turn to meet her match in a thrilling showdown. Elegant, clever and wedded to her career, India is about to find herself locked in a clash of wills with the irresistible Jordan Farraday. A power struggle in the boardroom and…out of it….

With love,

Liz Fielding

Liz Fielding is the winner of the 2001 RITA® Award for Best Traditional Romance. To find out more about the author, visit her Web site at www.lizfielding.com

LIZ FIELDING

The Tycoon's Takeover

TORONTO • NEW YORK • LONDON
AMSTERDAM • PARIS • SYDNEY • HAMBURG
STOCKHOLM • ATHENS • TOKYO • MILAN • MADRID
PRAGUE • WARSAW • BUDAPEST • AUCKLAND

ISBN 0-373-03708-2

THE TYCOON'S TAKEOVER

First North American Publication 2002.

This edition published by arrangement with Harlequin Books S.A.

Visit us at www.eHarlequin.com

Printed in U.S.A.

PROLOGUE

WHO GOT HITCHED, *CELEBRITY* magazine

SECRET WEDDING IN SAMARINDA

Samarinda, fast becoming the 'must go' destination for those seeking a get-away-from-it-all break, was host to a very private wedding ceremony for Flora Claibourne and Bram Farraday Gifford last week. These charming pictures show the happy couple taking their vows in the stunning setting of the Royal Botanical Gardens, surrounded by wild vanilla orchids, a feature of this delightful venue.

This is the second Claibourne/Farraday wedding in as many months. Forebears of the two families founded London's favourite department store in the nineteenth century, but relations between them, at times, been reduced to near feud status over control of the store.

The new generation, however, have refreshingly decided that it's better to make love than war. Flora's younger sister, Romana, and Bram's cousin, Niall Farraday Macaulay, were married recently in Las Vegas.

We look forward to a new era of co-operation at Claibourne & Farraday, and wish both couples every happiness.

CITY DIARY, LONDON EVENING POST

Another Claibourne/Farraday merger.

There's a new spirit of co-operation abroad at London's

oldest department store, Claibourne & Farraday. The present generation of the two founding families—who famously never talk to one another—are doing more than talk as they finally meet face to face to thrash out the future of the company in the new century. The marriages between the two younger Claibourne sisters and Farraday heirs have been quiet affairs, however, suggesting that nothing is yet settled at the top.

India Claibourne is still Managing Director, and my sources suggest that Jordan Farraday is determined to supplant her in the immediate future. We'll be following events at the store with close interest.

CHAPTER ONE

'HAVE you seen this, JD?'

Jordan Farraday turned from the e-mail that had just arrived in his inbox. His secretary was offering him a magazine, folded back at the 'Who Got Hitched' page. 'You read *Celebrity* magazine, Christine? I had no idea you were that interested in the loves and lives of the rich and famous.'

'I live in hopes of seeing you in there one of these days,' she replied, as he took the magazine from her. 'Having a little fun.' Then, 'I wasn't sure if you knew.' She paused. 'You didn't say anything.'

'I knew.' He glanced at the photograph of his cousin, caught at the moment he placed a wedding ring on Flora Claibourne's finger, and felt an unexpected pang of something he couldn't quite identify. Envy? It was ridiculous—and yet Bram looked different...complete. As if he'd found something he'd been looking for all his life. Nonsense, of course. It was just the reflected glow of satisfaction from a woman who'd got exactly what she wanted. 'There's a paragraph in the late edition of the *Evening Post*,' he said. 'Presumably they picked it up from this.'

'Bram didn't call you? Before? After?'

He looked up, a wry smile twisting his mouth. 'Would you?'

She shook her head. 'Those Claibourne girls are quite something. I wonder what they use?'

'Use?'

'Spells, charms, love potions…' she offered. 'I'd have said that your cousins were two of the most unlikely marriage prospects in London.' Then, with a slight gesture that deferred to him, 'After you.'

'Thank you,' he said drily.

'Yet first Niall and now Bram have succumbed with a speed that suggests something added to the water.'

'Grief fades in time. The playboy life loses its charm. They were ready to fall in love,' he said dismissively. 'My mistake was to put them in close contact with two of the most interesting women in London.'

'And you're about to spend a month in the company of interesting woman number three. Their big sister. The boss lady who's presumably taught them everything they know. Are you crazy?'

'No, Christine, single-minded.' He glanced again at the photograph. 'Unlike my cousins, who seem to have had other things on their minds, regaining control of a department store is my priority. At the end of the month I shall have done just that.'

'You don't need to shadow India Claibourne for five minutes, let alone a month, to achieve that.'

'No,' he agreed, 'I don't. But it's polite to give the lady a chance to make her case.'

'Rubbish.' Her eyes narrowed. 'You're up to something.' And when he didn't bother to deny it, she said, 'It'll all end in tears.'

'That,' he said, 'is the plan.'

'If you're suggesting they'll be her tears, I think you

should go back to the drawing board,' she said, retrieving the magazine and holding up the picture as a warning. 'Consider what happened to your cousins when they got involved with the Claibourne girls.'

'That was just a sideshow, Christine. This is the main event.'

'You're playing with fire.'

'It wouldn't be the first time,' he pointed out.

'When it comes to taking a chance with money, I'd put my last silk shirt on you. This is different.'

'Are you suggesting that I don't know what I'm doing?'

'Heaven forbid,' she declared. 'I'm simply suggesting that if you value your freedom you should invent a crisis that requires your presence on the other side of the world for the next month. Leave the Claibourne & Farraday business to the lawyers.'

'Bolt for cover? And have the *City Diary* editor amuse his readers with the suggestion that I'm running scared of India Claibourne? They would enjoy that.'

'There are worse things than being laughed at. Marriage isn't just a word, JD. It's a sentence. I know. I served nearly ten years before I managed to tunnel out.'

'Christine, we've worked together for a long time. You know me probably as well as anyone on this earth. Are you really suggesting that I won't be able to spend a few hours in the company of India Claibourne without falling so hopelessly in love with her that I'll be on my knees within the month?'

'Accounts are already organising a sweepstake on how long you'll last,' she replied.

It did not escape his notice that she hadn't answered

his question. But then she didn't know the full history. For his cousins control of Claibourne & Farraday was just good business. For him it was personal. Deeply personal.

This wasn't just about a department store. That was the public dispute, one that had been thoroughly rehearsed thirty years earlier, and the outcome was a foregone conclusion—as India Claibourne must know. Her father must have warned her that she couldn't win, but she was stubbornly refusing to accept the inevitable, refusing to play by the rules.

He wasn't taken in for a minute by her invitation for him and his cousins to spend time at the store, to 'shadow' her and her sisters, see how the store was run in this high-tech media age. She was just playing for time while she and her lawyers tried to find some loophole in the partnership agreement that would allow her to remain in control.

Not that he was complaining. If he'd planned it himself, it couldn't have worked out better.

That he would take over from Peter Claibourne now that he'd retired was inevitable. India Claibourne's decision to put up a fight, giving Jordan the opportunity to reverse history, humiliate her as her father had humiliated his mother, was icing spread thickly on the cake.

Christine was still waiting for some response, he realised. 'A sweepstake?' he repeated. 'On what, exactly?'

'On how many days it will be before you, um, get down on your knees.'

'My knees? And why would I do that?'

'To propose to the lady. Beg her to marry you.'

'Oh, please!'

'I realise that's an alien concept for a man of your

wealth, name and all-round fanciability. But it cannot have escaped your notice that she's got a matching set.'

No, it hadn't escaped his notice. India Claibourne was as lovely as she was rich. But she had one fatal weakness: she'd do anything to keep control of Claibourne & Farraday. 'And a proposal would be enough, would it? For some lucky soul to win this sweepstake?'

'A diamond on the lady's finger is one option,' she admitted. 'But the hot ticket is for a wedding.'

'Within a month? How likely is that?'

She held up one finger. 'Niall Farraday Macaulay married Romana Claibourne in Las Vegas on Day 29.' A second finger. 'Bram Farraday Gifford married Flora Claibourne in Saraminda on Day 30. I'm sure that anything they can do, you can do better.' Then, with a grin, 'Three's a charm, JD.'

'Is that so?' He shrugged. 'Well, here's the word from the horse's mouth. If you've got money to waste on such nonsense, make sure you draw the number with "No Wedding" written next to it. Believe me, whatever gossip you may read in your magazine, it'll take more than a seductive smile to get me in front of a registrar.'

'The lady *has* more. A whole department store more. Why don't you save time—and lawyers' fees—and propose a dynastic marriage? That way you both win. You have to admit that she'd make any man a stunning consort.'

'I'm admitting nothing. And I thought you were opposed to marriage on principle?'

'Arranged marriages are different. The participants have more realistic expectations. And this would be more like an advantageous merger of two companies—something you know all about.' Taken with the idea, she went on, 'I can't understand why it hasn't happened before—in the days when marriages were arranged for gain, rather than left to chance. The families must have been close at one time.'

'There has been quite enough dynastic marriage-making in the last few weeks without me joining in. And I don't need a consort, no matter how stunning she is. All I need is for the Claibournes to hand over what is rightfully mine with the minimum of fuss.'

'If it was minimum fuss you wanted you'd have sent in the lawyers two months ago. You want something else, and I have no doubt you'll get it. I just hope it makes you happy.' Then, 'But don't eat or drink anything while you're at the store. Oh, and don't, whatever else you do, get a haircut in the salon.' And she grinned. 'Just in case India Claibourne uses hair clippings to cast her spells.'

'I'm sure you've got something important to be getting on with while I'm making my presence felt at London's favourite department store tomorrow, Christine. Swapping knitting patterns, perhaps? Or phoning your daughter to discuss her latest pregnancy?' he suggested, signalling that as far as he was concerned that particular subject was now closed.

'Don't do it, JD,' she said, not in the least bit intimidated. But then he hadn't expected her to be.

'Or maybe you should give careful thought to the possibility of taking early retirement and becoming a full-time grandmother,' he continued, his expression still in neutral. 'I could get one of those sexy girls with long legs and a degree in Business Studies to replace you.'

'You wouldn't do that.'

'Oh? And why not?'

'Precisely because I'm not sexy. I'm safely middle-aged, plump and motherly,' she said, heading back to her own office. 'You know I'm not going to fall in love with you and make life difficult in the office. I'm also the best secretary in the world. Probably.' When she reached the door, however, she paused and looked back at him. 'Twenty-one days,' she said. 'If she gets you on Day 21, I win the sweep.'

'Try and get your money back,' he suggested. 'Sell your ticket to someone really gullible.'

'Goodnight, JD. Don't work too late. All work and no play…' She left the proverb hanging, closing the door gently behind her as she left for the night, and he finally smiled. She might be talking rubbish about India Claibourne, but she was right about one thing. She was the best secretary he'd ever known and he wouldn't be trading her in for a younger model any time soon. Then, as he turned back to his PC and the e-mail from India Claibourne, his smile faded. It wasn't long. Just one line. It said:

Two down, one to go. Are you ready to quit, Mr Farraday?

Clearly she'd been afraid that with his advance guard neutralised by her lovely sisters he might change his mind about shadowing her during June. This was a 'dare-you' challenge to his masculine pride.

Christine was wrong, he decided as he switched off the screen. He wasn't the one playing with fire. It was India

Claibourne who was about to get her fingers...and anything else she cared to risk...burned.

India Claibourne paused in front of the department store that had borne her family name for nearly two centuries and looked up.

Claibourne & Farraday.

A byword for class and style. The name said it all.

In fact it said rather too much.

The Farraday grated. A lot. Their silent partners hadn't done much—other than accumulate capital and take their share of the profits—in living memory. Her living memory, anyway.

She didn't have a problem with that. They were equal partners and were entitled to their share of the profits—welcome to them—as long as they kept out of her way. But they weren't keeping out of her way. Since her father's sudden retirement, following his heart attack, they had become disturbingly vocal.

'Good morning, Miss India.' The commissionaire tipped his top hat to her.

'Good morning, Mr Edwards.' She paused, stepping to one side, out of the way of early arrivals at the store. 'The customers seem eager this morning.'

'Summer is always busy, miss. London is full of visitors and they all come to Claibourne's.'

She smiled at the way he automatically shortened the name.

Claibourne's.

It had a ring to it. It was easy to say. And once she'd seen off Jordan Farraday that was what the store would become. Claibourne's.

No more Farradays. Ever.

'My wife showed me the wedding picture of Miss Flora in *Celebrity* magazine last night,' he continued, as she lingered at the entrance, her fertile imagination supplying a pleasing picture of the frontage with just one name above the door. 'She looked quite radiant. It's wonderful for the store...both Miss Romana and Miss Flora marrying Farradays.'

Which brought her swiftly back to reality. Jordan Farraday's advance guard, his cousins and partners in his bid to take over control of the store, were now her brothers-in-law.

Her delaying tactics—having the Farradays shadow them to see what running a department store actually entailed—had backfired. Badly.

But she smiled nonetheless. 'It's very exciting for them. For all of us. I wish I could have been with them.' Her sisters, however, having fallen under the Farraday spell, had chosen to get married first and only tell their families afterwards. Or, in Flora's case, leave them to find out like everyone else when they read it in the newspaper.

She couldn't fault their reasoning. In their shoes, she'd have done the same.

Meanwhile they were all wisely keeping their heads down in their honeymoon hideaways, leaving the field clear for the main battle.

It was between her and Jordan Farraday now. But then, it always was going to be between the two of them. She was in control of the store, sitting in the seat he believed to be rightfully his.

Her sisters, his cousins, were interested parties. But she and Jordan were the ones with the most to gain—or lose.

She had one month left—this month—to show him that if the Farradays thought they could run Claibourne & Farraday in their spare time they were wrong. This was no longer an emporium for gentlemen, a place where the customers were all known personally.

Her father had continued to think of it that way long after reality had suggested otherwise. But she had hauled it into the modern era and, now he'd retired, the sky was the limit. But first she had to see off the Farradays. More specifically, she had to see off Jordan David Farraday.

It shouldn't be difficult. The man was a venture capitalist, not a retailer. He really couldn't want to take on something so time-consuming. It was control he wanted. The last word. At least she hoped that was all he wanted. A prime site, the name alone, would be a big prize for one of the retail chains. But he wouldn't...couldn't...

A shiver, as if someone had walked over her grave, goosed her flesh.

Jordan Farraday showed his pass at the rear entrance of the building, parked his sports car in the space that had been allocated to him, then asked the security guard at the staff entrance to ring through to India Claibourne's office to let her know he'd arrived.

She wasn't there.

'Will you pass on my best wishes when you speak to her?' India, dragging her mind back from a nightmare vision of the plans Jordan Farraday might have for the store, glanced at the commissionaire. 'Miss Flora,' he prompted as he opened the door for her. 'I hope she'll be very happy.'

'Thank you, Mr Edwards. I'll tell her.'

Most days she used the staff entrance at the rear of the store, but occasionally, having parked her car, she took the time to walk around to the main entrance, look at the window displays and enter the store as if she were a customer. Remind herself of that first time when, four years old, she'd been brought to the store by her grandmother to visit Santa's grotto and had believed she'd walked into the Aladdin's cave in her storybook.

As she walked into the marble and mahogany entrance hall, spangled with coloured light from the Tiffany stained glass window that rose up three floors through the stairwell, the rush of excitement, the sense of wonder was as powerful as ever.

She would not give this up for anything. Ever.

But it occurred to her that sitting in her office waiting for Jordan Farraday to turn up and take it away from her was entirely the wrong strategy. Romana had dragged Niall off to a charity bungee jump. Bram had been given no choice but to join Flora on a research trip to a tropical island.

Neither of them had had time to draw breath, settle into the standard 'I'm a man and I know best' routine.

They hadn't known what had hit them until it was too late. She had to ensure that for the next month she was the one in front and Farraday was always following her. If he ever turned the tables and took the lead it would all be over.

Sitting at her desk going over last month's sales figures when—if—he responded to the challenge in her incendiary e-mail wouldn't fit the bill. He'd be expecting that and he wouldn't be impressed by her ability to read a balance sheet.

She had to be doing something that was totally outside his normal experience. Something that would give her an advantage. With a whole department store to play with, it shouldn't be that difficult.

She glanced at the noticeboard listing the special events taking place in the store that day. An all-day specialist doll collectors' fair in the gallery. A cookery demonstration, with a celebrity chef doing his stuff, in the food hall at lunchtime. A book-signing by a well known American author in the country to promote her newest blockbuster novel. Bags of opportunities for photographs, she thought as she took the lift to the top-floor office suite.

She needed to keep her photograph in the papers. Remind everyone that she was running the show. She'd get Molly in the PR department on to that, as her sister was away. The lift door opened to dust sheets and the sound of hammering, and she smiled a little grimly as she crossed to her office.

Jordan Farraday might be sharing it with her for the next month, but he wouldn't enjoy the experience much.

'Indie…' Her PA appeared in the doorway. 'We've got a small problem in the nursery department.'

'How small?'

'Baby-sized. One of our customers left it a little late to do her shopping and she's gone into labour. The paramedics have arrived, and they'll be moving her to hospital as soon as they can, but I thought you'd want to know.'

'I'd better go down there—make sure everything possible is being done.'

'Well, actually…' India paused on her way out. 'There's no need.'

'No need?'

'It's being taken care of. Since you weren't here, JD took charge—'

'JD?' India frowned.

'Jordan Farraday. His staff call him JD, he said.'

'Jordan Farraday? He's here already? In the store?' Her mouth was working on automatic, she realised. A bit like a goldfish, and making about as much sense. Of course he was here.

She'd been mentally redesigning the frontage, chatting with the commissionaire, taking her morning stroll through the main selling floors while Jordan David Farraday had gone straight to the top floor and was already taking over her job.

'He arrived on the dot of ten o'clock. You said you were expecting him some time today, so when Security buzzed through I told them to send him up.'

'I was expecting him to ring and let me know when he was coming. I wasn't expecting him to just turn up…unannounced!'

'I was supposed to say, Go away, we aren't ready for you?' India raised a hand in a gesture of apology, shook her head. 'I gave him coffee and put him in your office. There is nowhere else,' she complained.

No, there was nowhere else. It had seemed like a great idea when Romana suggested ripping out underused offices and moving Customer Services to the top floor in order to create more selling space. And why hang about? Get in the builders, create a noisy, dusty atmosphere and maybe, without an office—or even a desk—to call his own, JD Farraday would be less inclined to linger in the store. It was time she needed. Not her arch-nemesis following her every move.

'I'm sorry, Sally. You did the right thing, of course, but just because he was sitting in my office did you have to treat the man as if he were already running the place? Did you have to tell him about the population explosion in the nursery department?'

'I didn't. Someone came rushing in with the news and he just sort of...well...took charge,' she said, a little breathlessly.

'Great.' She took a deep breath. 'But I really do think I'd better go and see what's happening downstairs.' She was in no rush. In fact she had a sudden craving to be somewhere else. Lying on a deserted beach, perhaps. 'Do you ever just wish the alarm clock hadn't gone off? That you'd slept through the day?'

'Not this one, I promise you. JD Farraday is not a man I'd ever want to miss.'

'That's all I need. A secretary with a crush on a man who wants to take over my store.'

'His name is above the door too. And I don't have a crush. My personal life is fully spoken for.' Then she grinned. 'But I'm not dead.'

'That'll be a comfort to you when he's sitting in my chair and you're looking for a new job.'

'Oh, come on. That's never going to happen.'

'Two months ago I might have agreed with you.' Suddenly she wasn't so sure. Her fallback position was the equal opportunities argument. He had a centuries-old agreement stating that control should pass to the 'oldest male'. She was basing her equality on being 'oldest female'. Would a lot of old men in wigs be swayed by the logic of that argument? Or would they—as she suspected—go for just plain 'oldest'. Farraday, after all, was a man with a track record for making money. All she had to offer was a lifetime's knowledge of the business and a passion to turn Claibourne's into a household name—not just in London, or Britain, but in the world.

'Hey, if all else fails you can always do a Claibourne on him.'

Dragged back from the yawning chasm of failure, she frowned. 'A Claibourne?'

'Flutter those long dark lashes at him. Once he's in love, he'll forget all about taking away your toy.'

'Oh, great. I'm trying to convince everyone that I can run this store on merit and you want me to seduce the man. Whatever happened to thirty years of women's liberation?' As she turned angrily away she snagged her tights on a battered cardboard box. Great. The day that she'd begun with an uneasy feeling of foreboding was rapidly going downhill. 'Sally, what the devil is this?'

'Oh—' She sucked in her teeth as she saw the damage to India's tights, took a new pair from a supply she kept in her bottom drawer and handed them over. 'Sorry. The builders left it there. They're files from your father's office. Pretty old stuff, but I thought you might want to look at them before I sent them down to the basement.'

'But I cleaned out all the filing cabinets in Dad's office.'

'These were right at the back of that big walk-in cupboard. It looked like a box of old catalogues, but, knowing how disorganised your father was, I thought I'd better check before it went down the chute into the skip. The files were at the bottom.'

India flicked through the top file. Thirty years old, it dated from the time her father had taken over the store from JD Farraday's grandfather, and her scalp prickled with a rush of excitement. 'Sally, that designer skirt you've been drooling over...it's yours. Charge it to my account.' Cutting off her thanks, she went on, 'Just shift these files first,' she said, peeling off the torn tights and replacing them. 'I'd hate JD Farraday to fall over them and sue us.'

'Why would he do that? Wouldn't that be like suing himself?' Then, realising that it was not a conversation with a future, she said, 'I'll put them in your office.'

'No!' India took a deep breath. 'No, don't do that. Arrange for them to be put in my car.' The last thing she needed was Jordan Farraday looking over her shoulder as she went through them.

Correction. The last thing she needed was Jordan Farraday. Full stop.

CHAPTER TWO

INDIA took another deep breath before she pushed open the door to the nursery department. She seemed to be doing that a lot this morning, but it was fortunate that her lungs were loaded with air, because she didn't breathe again for what seemed like an age.

JD Farraday was the kind of man who would always make the need to breathe redundant.

He didn't court publicity, but she'd gathered what information she could about the man. The grainy photographs from the financial pages of heavyweight newspapers had suggested an averagely good-looking, dark-haired man in his mid to late thirties. They didn't do him justice. There was nothing average about Jordan Farraday.

His features were arranged in the conventional manner, it was true, but the combination achieved something far from ordinary. There was something about him that transcended mere good looks.

As if that were not enough he was taller, his hair darker—the touch of silver at his temple only emphasising just how dark—than just tall, or just dark. But that was the superficial, obvious stuff.

What set her midriff trembling like a joke jelly, prickled her scalp and set up the tiny hairs on her skin, was the way he dominated the room, the way every person in it was looking to him for guidance, leadership.

Jordan Farraday was the archetypal dominant male. Alpha man. Leader of the pack. The kind of man who would always make other men appear ordinary, who would attract women like iron filings to a magnet. In short, he was the most exciting man she'd set eyes on in months…years… possibly ever…

And she'd taken him on in a winner-takes-all battle for control of Claibourne & Farraday.

Not that he appeared in the least bit threatening at the moment. Far from it. As she stood there he crouched down to gently sandwich the hand of the very young soon-to-be-mother between both of his, reassuring her as she was fastened into a chair trolley by a paramedic, his smile a promise that he would let nothing bad happen to her.

'You're going to be fine, Serena. I've phoned your boyfriend and he's going straight to the hospital.' His voice was low, calming, like being stroked by velvet. 'He'll be waiting for you when you arrive.' He glanced at the paramedics. 'Ready?' One of them nodded. 'You'll be there in just a few minutes.' As he turned slightly the light behind him lit up a classic profile—the kind that Greek sculptors had reserved for gods. 'Would you like me to come along with you in the ambulance?'

By way of reply, the mother-to-be gripped his hand more tightly. 'My bags…' she began, less concerned with the swoon quotient of the man at her side, apparently, than the fate of her shopping. But then she was in labour—and India caught her breath again as the woman was seized by a contraction.

In her place, she probably wouldn't give a damn about how good-looking a man was either. She swallowed. In her place, she'd want someone exactly like Jordan Farraday holding her hand…

He glanced around. A few feet away a hovering assistant was holding a couple of bags, and as he straightened to take them he saw her standing in the doorway. For a moment he remained perfectly still as their gazes locked, held, and for a long moment she was his prisoner.

'Miss Claibourne…' She jumped at the sound of her name and the moment passed as the department manager came between them. 'We've had quite a morning.'

'So I see,' she said, making an effort to give the woman her full attention, despite the charged feeling at the back of her neck that suggested JD Farraday's gaze was still fastened firmly upon her. 'It appears one of our customers left her shopping trip rather late.'

'Well, no harm done. Mr Farraday has been wonderful. He calmed that silly girl when no one else could.' India thought that was probably a first. It seemed unlikely that was his usual effect on girls—or women—of any description. 'Then he phoned her boyfriend, and when people wouldn't move away he sent them all over to the coffee shop for complimentary coffee and cakes.'

About to ask why it had been left to him, why the manager hadn't done all that herself, she bit back her irritation at the woman's ineffectiveness, and her lack of sympathy, and concerned herself with the fact that Jordan Farraday had witnessed it and taken charge.

So much for throwing him off balance.

It was not a great start.

'I hope it was all right to do that?' the woman added uncertainly, when India didn't immediately respond.

'Absolutely right,' she said, discovering for herself

what the expression 'through gritted teeth' actually meant. 'Should anything like this happen again, don't hesitate to do that,' she said, and made a mental note to have the training department bring it up at the weekly workshops they ran for the managerial staff. With a reminder not to refer to the customers as 'silly' under any circumstances.

'Miss Claibourne.' The quiet authority of his voice matched his appearance. Just the way he said her name necessitated another deep breath before she turned to confront JD Farraday.

'Mr Farraday.' She extended her hand in a manner she hoped was sufficiently businesslike to counteract the breathlessness of her voice. Perhaps it didn't matter. If her reaction—and she was famously difficult to impress—was anything to go by, he must believe that all women were chronically breathless. 'I had assumed you'd call before you arrived, or I would have come straight up to my office instead of taking my usual morning walk through the store.' She glanced at the mother-to-be, who was rapidly disappearing behind the door of the goods lift. 'You seem to have kept yourself busy, however.'

'It's been an interesting morning,' he admitted.

'A little different from your office in the City.'

'We do have women in the City. Some of them even have babies, although we do encourage them to take maternity leave rather than have them in the office.' She'd expected him to be dour, cool. He was the enemy, after all. They both knew that. Yet his wry smile indicated a sense of humour, and the firm manner with which he clasped her hand, held it, suggested that he'd waited all his life to meet her.

Making a determined effort to collect herself, she retrieved it. 'We'd rather they didn't do it here either,' she admitted. 'But there's nothing like being thrown in at the deep end. Since I arrived too late to do anything more than hold things up I thought it best to leave you to it. You seemed to be managing,' she added, in another of those 'gritted teeth' moments. Then, 'I was under the impression that you were going to be holding the young lady's hand while she's whizzed through the traffic to the hospital.'

'I thought someone should offer,' he replied. As a criticism of her department manager's ineffectuality it was masterly in its understatement. 'However, the paramedics were kind enough to assure me that I'd be in the way. They suggested I might to go along later—with her shopping.' He held up a couple of their trademark dark red glossy carrier bags, the store's name printed in elegant copperplate gold lettering. She had a momentary flash of her vision of the way it would be—Claibourne's, all in lower-case modern type—once she'd seen him off. 'They didn't seem to think she'd have much use for it in the next hour or so.'

'What? Oh, no, I imagine not.' She looked around. 'Excuse me.' The assistants were busy returning the department to normal, and she crossed to thank them for the way they'd handled a difficult situation.

'You will let us know what happens, won't you, Miss Claibourne?'

'Of course. Maybe you'd like to choose a card and sign it from everyone in the department? I'll phone the hospital later, and when we know that everything has gone smoothly I'll take it to the hospital with some flowers. And her shopping. Maybe one of you would be kind enough to take it up to my office?' She turned to JD Farraday. 'Or maybe you'd prefer to go on behalf of the store?' she offered. 'See the job through?'

'Since I'm spending the next month observing you at work, Miss Claibourne, I think you should give her the flowers,' he said, surrendering the bags to a blushing assistant. 'While I watch.'

Before she could quite make up her mind whether he was being serious or sarcastic, he smiled, which short-circuited any but the most positive thoughts, making it difficult to remember that it was her intention to spend as little time as possible in his company.

'If you've nothing more pressing this evening, of course you're most welcome to join me. But it's not compulsory. Even a ''shadow'' has statutory rights regarding working hours,' she said, making an effort to keep things cool and businesslike. Then she spoiled it all by smiling right back. 'Excuse me, I'd better just go and let everyone know they can resume shopping.'

For a moment, the space of a heartbeat, as he'd looked up and seen India Claibourne standing in the doorway watching him, Jordan had known he'd made a mistake. That his secretary had been right and that he was playing with fire. That he should run, not walk away from this woman.

He already knew she was lovely. Every single photograph of her, since her first photo-call at the age of four, sitting on Santa's knee in the C&F Christmas grotto, had been filed away with the newspaper articles on the store supplied by a cuttings agency.

With her little cap of dark hair cut into a neat fringe,

her eyes huge with the excitement of it all, there had been the promise of beauty even then.

As she'd grown into a lively teenager, a dashing young woman, her face had changed from that of a round-cheeked child into the fine-boned elegance of genuine beauty. One with style, class and the indefinable something extra which made a woman special: the something extra that reminded a man there was more to life than making money.

Only her eyes had never changed. They were still huge, eager, burning with life, and for a moment the heat they generated had seared him in a vivid affirmation of Christine's warning on the dangers of playing with fire.

Then she'd turned away to speak to her department manager and common sense had kicked in.

He was that rarest of commodities, a wealthy bachelor. His world had never been short of lovely women. But he hadn't lost his head over one of them yet, and there was absolutely no chance of him losing it over India Claibourne.

That wasn't his plan at all. In this relationship there would be only one loser.

For a moment he watched her walk across the sales floor towards the coffee shop. Tall, willowy, her long legs emphasised by high, high heels, her elegant figure merely sketched at by the suit she was wearing. Burgundy-red, rich and dark and expensive, with discreet gold buttons. Claibourne & Farraday's livery colours.

That she'd chosen to wear it today in order to make some kind of statement he never doubted for a second.

She'd fight him for possession of her domain with her last breath. The knowledge sent a ripple of excitement through him that was far more pleasing than all his cold, calculating plans.

Before the month was up she would surrender everything to him. More than surrender. She was the one playing with fire and she was going to get burned.

And with that pleasing thought he went after her.

'Ladies, gentlemen…' She didn't raise her voice, or rap on a table, yet there was an immediate hush in the coffee shop, a tribute to a presence that was rare in a woman. Confidence, self-belief, a power that came from within. She was a worthy adversary. 'I just wanted to thank you all for your patience. You can continue with your shopping whenever you're ready.' For a moment she was deluged with questions about the young mother-to-be. 'I'll be calling the hospital later for news of our newest customer,' she continued, 'and if the parents give their permission we'll post news of the birth on our website.' Then, checking her watch, she turned to him and said, 'I have to go. I've got an author arriving for a book-signing in a few minutes.'

'I saw the posters when I arrived. Is it simply a meet-and-greet? Or will you have to stand by and hand her an endless supply of pens?'

'She can manage her own pens, but she does merit the full red carpet treatment. Fortunately she doesn't have time for lunch today.' Then, 'Or maybe I make a less attractive lunchtime companion than my father. He always took her to the Ritz and plied her with champagne,' she added, with a sideways glance from beneath dark glossy lashes that appeared to suggest that if he took over he'd have that pleasure to look forward to.

'You could do that.'

'I don't think either the Ritz or the champagne would make up for my father not being there to flirt with her.'

'He's certainly had plenty of practice,' he agreed blandly. Then, as her cheekbones flushed pink with anger, 'I'd have doubted a book department was a cost-effective use of space these days,' he said as they both reached out to press the button to summon the lift. He beat her to it by a fraction of a second, and their fingers tangled momentarily before she snatched them back, as if stung. Her nails were polished the same deep burgundy-red as her suit. As her smooth, soft lips. 'Can you compete with the big book chains?' he enquired, making an effort to concentrate on business.

'The decision to close the book department was made several weeks ago,' she replied. Again that little sideways flicker of eyelashes. This time they said, *You see? I'm one step ahead of you.* 'It's part of the rationalisation of floor space that's in progress at the moment. We've started on the top floor, as you must have noticed.'

'Impossible to miss,' he agreed. 'It must make concentration difficult.'

'I never have any difficulty in concentrating on the important stuff.' The lift arrived and they got in. 'Ground floor, please,' she said, abandoning competition in favour of making it appear that he was at her beck and call. He pressed the button that would take them to the ground floor without comment. She was, he had to admit, a fast learner. 'We're reducing the office area by half. My father has retired...' she glanced at him '...but then you know that.' She paused momentarily, as if expecting him to enquire after the man's health. When he didn't, she went on, 'And Flora rarely uses her office, so they are both being ripped out. Romana's office is being remodelled to provide space for the two of us—the centre partition will be movable, for full-scale planning meetings. Once that's done, my office will go too.'

'May I see the plans? I'd like to know what you're doing with the space you've made. The reasoning behind the changes. When you have a moment.'

'I'd be delighted to explain what we're doing, Mr Farraday. Just as long as you accept that I'm extending you a courtesy, not seeking your approval.'

'Of course. Control is absolute. We both understand that.' He certainly wouldn't be seeking approval from the Claibournes for *his* plans. Their helpless howls of rage as he sold the store would only sweeten his triumph.

They reached the ground floor and he followed her across the entrance lobby to the main door, where a staff photographer was waiting, along with a group of fans eager to catch the first glimpse of their idol. 'Any sign of her, Mr Edwards?' she asked the commissionaire.

'She's stopped just down there at the traffic lights. You've got about thirty seconds.'

'The white stretch limo,' she explained. 'The lady is a celebrity. She likes to make an entrance.' Then, 'Maybe we'll have a little time between the book-signing and the celebrity chef.'

'Celebrity chef?'

'In the food hall at twelve o'clock. He's making some Italian dish to promote a new product line. I'm afraid you've chosen a rather hectic day to visit us, but maybe we can find some time to look at the plans before he arrives.'

He didn't miss her suggestion that he was 'visiting'.

That this was her territory. 'Perhaps you'd be good enough to run the programme for the rest of the month by me too,' he said, reminding her that his visit wasn't a day-trip. 'When you have a moment.'

'I'm sorry. This must seem very tedious to you. But a store of this size needs to provide constant entertainment value—something to draw the crowds.'

'And you keep a very high profile.'

'It's not the way you do things in your world, I know, but then high finance is, by its very nature, a secretive business.'

'I think the word you want is *confidential*.'

'Is there a difference?' She glanced up at him with those cool dark eyes. 'Apart from tone?'

Not that much in the meaning, perhaps, but in the dismissive manner in which she said it there was a world of difference. 'Tone is everything.'

'Perhaps. This is different. Every day is showtime, and since it's my name above the door I have to be centre stage.' Meaning that he'd have to be front and centre too, when he took over? 'Our customers like the fact that if something goes wrong I'm here, not hidden away in some anonymous head office.'

Again there was the slightest pause, as if she expected him to say something. Did she really expect him to comment? Promise that he'd be on call for any customer with a complaint? She did something with her shoulders. Nothing as definitive as a shrug, but it made its point loud and clear. It said that he didn't measure up to her ideal of a CEO for Claibourne & Farraday. It was a situation that she apparently found immeasurably satisfying, if the small smile tucking up the corners of her mouth was anything to judge by.

'I'll check my diary,' she continued. 'I might have that ''moment'' to run through the event schedule later. Of course there's nothing stopping you from picking up a programme at the information desk. Or even going to the website to check it out for yourself.'

'Like your customers, I prefer the personal touch. You can tell me all about it this evening.' Which dealt with her smile, reducing it to a puzzled frown. 'After we've visited the hospital. Over dinner, perhaps?' Then, almost as an afterthought, 'You do manage to find a little time to eat?'

'Yes, but—'

'I've cleared my diary in order to indulge you, Miss Claibourne. I think I'm entitled to a little consideration in return.'

'India, honey!' Before she could respond, she was enveloped in the warm embrace of her guest.

India greeted the exuberant author with more than usual warmth. She deserved it for rescuing her from having to cope with a remark that she suspected had been finely judged to wind her up.

He'd *indulged* her?

He made her sound like some wilful little girl, who'd been given her own way under sufferance, but who would shortly be sent to bed unless she was very, very good.

And then the author spotted him, and lit up like the Christmas tree in Trafalgar Square. 'Who,' she demanded, 'is this beautiful man?'

India was about to introduce them, and invite Mr

Farraday to escort the lady novelist up to the book department, when the beautiful man in question pre-empted her. 'Farraday,' he said, taking her hand with a dazzling smile. 'Jordan Farraday.'

She laughed. 'You mean I get a Claibourne *and* a Farraday? This is so special!' As she turned to face the cameras for the PR shots she snuggled up to him, before taking his arm and sweeping towards the escalator, leaving India trailing in their wake.

'We should have lunch, Mr Farraday,' she said, as they arrived at the book department and she finally released him.

'How I wish that were possible,' he said, with every appearance of deepest regret. 'Another time, perhaps.' He looked around at the queue of women clutching copies of her book to be signed. 'I appear to be keeping you from your fans.' And with that he gave India a look that seemed to say, *Well? How did I do? Could Peter Claibourne have done it better?* And the answer, of course, was no. Then he glanced at his wristwatch. 'If you'll excuse me?' Then, to India, 'I need to make a phone call.'

'Please, use my office.'

She could have gone with him, but she was glad of a moment to herself. She wasn't taking anything for granted, however, and used the internal phone to call Sally.

'Mr Farraday is on his way up. You can give him the event list for June, but he isn't to see the new office plans. Or anything else.'

'Anything?' Sally replied, with a throaty chuckle.

A distraction in the form of her sexy secretary, whose

highest ambition was to flirt for her country in the Olympic Games, might be useful, but try as she might she couldn't summon up any enthusiasm for the idea. Instead, rather lamely, she said, 'Oh, *please*...'

She couldn't quite understand why the idea bothered her, and she put it firmly out of her mind, returning to pose for photographs for the website with the author and some of her fans.

After that there was nothing to stop her going back to her office and rejoining her shadow. The temptation to go down to the archives—a place where she could not be found unless she wanted to be—and hide out for the rest of the day was compelling.

She pushed open the door to the stairs. Up or down?

She'd never know, because Jordan Farraday was leaning, one shoulder against the wall, legs casually crossed, cutting off any chance of escape. She jumped nervously, and to cover her reaction laughed. 'Mr Farraday. I thought you were using my office to make your phone call.'

'I didn't need a desk and I have my mobile.'

'In other words it was simply a device to escape being pressed into joining the lady for dinner instead?'

'I've already got a dinner date. With you.' And he dropped the cellphone he'd been using into his pocket. 'What next?'

'Coffee,' she said as, cut off from retreat, she took the stairs up to her office, cursing herself for not having thought of inviting the author to join them. She glanced back over her shoulder and found her eyes were on a level with his. They were dark as pitch and just as unfathomable. 'You wouldn't be able to walk away so easily if you were running the show.'

'When I'm running the show, Miss Claibourne, I'll pay someone else to play clown. I'd offer you the job, since you enjoy it so much, but somehow I don't think you'd want to work for me.'

Ignoring his comment about playing clown—but mentally filing away the fact that he planned on putting in a manager to use against him—she said, 'It would make better sense to leave things the way they are.'

'For you, maybe. Not for me. But you already know that.'

Yes. She knew. While her father had been running the store he'd been able to do whatever he wanted and all Jordan Farraday could do was stand by and watch. He wasn't going to leave things the way they were because he wanted that power for himself. Just for the sake of it? Or did he already have plans that he knew she wouldn't like?

'What time does your next party turn arrive?' he asked, interrupting this disturbing chain of thought.

'I wouldn't let our celebrity chef hear you describe him as a party turn. Not when he's got a knife in his hand.' She ran her swipe card through the security lock and swept through the door and down the corridor, stopping by Sally's office to ask for coffee and check for messages. 'And schedule a meeting for me with the training manager, will you, please? As a matter of urgency. That woman in the nursery department didn't cope well today.'

'She's just acting manager, isn't she? While the manager is on holiday?'

'Yes, and I'm afraid it showed. We need to make sure everyone knows how to deal with these one-off emergencies. We can't rely on Mr Farraday to be around to take charge and hold hands next time.' She glanced up, challenging him to admit it. Disconcertingly, he smiled, and for a moment she couldn't think what she'd been going to say next. 'And…um…'

'The hospital?' Sally prompted, flirting dangerously with an I-told-you-so smile.

'Check and see how our mother-to-be is doing. As soon as we've got a result I'll want flowers, and a basket of baby stuff in an appropriate colour. And a nice big C&F teddy. It'll look good in a photograph if they're prepared to do a PR piece. I'll want a photographer with me this evening when I visit—with luck we'll catch them on an emotional high that they want to share with the rest of the world.'

'I'll get onto it. We need to finalise the details of the retirement party for Maureen Derbyshire too, when you've got a minute.' And she turned to Jordan Farraday. 'Don't miss it, JD. It's going to be quite a party.'

'I fear Mr Farraday finds our small concerns rather dull, Sally,' she said, before he could respond. Then, turning to him, 'You wouldn't understand, Mr Farraday, but when Maureen leaves it'll be the end of an era. She started work here on the day she left school. Fifty years ago.'

'Then she must have known my grandfather.'

Damn! She hadn't thought of that. Point scoring off JD Farraday was going to be tricky. But she smiled and said, 'Yes, I imagine so.'

'I'm sure she'd be thrilled if you could find time to join us,' Sally said, innocent as a baby. 'It's on Thursday evening. In the Roof Garden Restaurant.'

'I'll be there,' he said, his gaze never leaving India's

face, mocking her as if, despite her secretary's invitation, he understood that she didn't want him popping up all over the place. 'On the understanding that India saves the first dance for me.'

CHAPTER THREE

'I CAN'T believe how young she is,' India said as they left the hospital early that evening. 'Or maybe I'm just getting old.'

'That must be it,' Jordan said. She glanced at him sharply and his eyes creased into the kind of smile designed to make a woman go weak at the knees. He was teasing her, she realised. Which was unexpected and had to be against the rules in a situation like this. But then Jordan Farraday undoubtedly made up the rules as he went along. 'What did you have to offer to get her to do those publicity shots?'

'That's confidential.' She'd taken a photographer with her, hoping to catch the new parents in a mood to share their news with the world. They had been. For a price. She and the new mother had done their deal in the man-free environment of the nappy-changing room. Serena hadn't wanted her boyfriend to know the details either. 'Between her and me.'

He raised his brows. 'That much?'

'She may be young, but she's not stupid.'

'Are you suggesting that she stage-managed the whole thing?'

'That she waited until the contractions were well established before taking a turn around the nursery department, you mean? That's very cynical of you, Mr Farraday. I was suggesting nothing of the kind. Simply that she understands the value of publicity.' She glanced up at him. 'You looked quite something with the new baby in your arms.'

'You pay and I get the publicity. It hardly seems fair.'

'The cost comes out of the PR budget,' she reminded him, trying to keep the edge out of her voice. Jordan Farraday was winning the publicity war hands down. First with the author, then making a hit with the celebrity chef, when he'd asked the kind of questions that made the man look like a towering culinary intellect. And then Serena had insisted he be the one to hold the baby. 'And *Claibourne's* gets the publicity.'

'In this instance it would seem that it's the "& Farraday" who'll get all the newspaper coverage.'

She shrugged as if it made no difference. 'It'll make a nice story,' she said. She'd like to believe his colleagues in the City would be ragging him about it for days, but had to admit that the prospect was unlikely. They'd more likely be awestruck by his ability to cope in the kind of crisis they'd never want to be anywhere near.

They'd taken a black cab to the hospital, to avoid the hassle of finding somewhere to park, and Jordan grabbed one now that was dropping off passengers. He spoke to the driver, then joined her in the back of the cab.

'Will we have the pleasure of your presence at the store tomorrow?' she asked.

'Today isn't over yet.'

'That's true,' she said, remembering the files in the boot of her car. 'I've got a load of paperwork to get through tonight.'

'Anything an interested shadow can help with?'

'No,' she said, too quickly. 'It's... Well...'

'Secret?' he offered.

'Confidential,' she said. 'Family business.'

'It's all family business,' he replied, as the cab pulled over to the kerb and came to a halt. 'One way or another. We're here.'

'Where?' India glanced out at the side street, where they had stopped in front of a small restaurant she knew by name, its reputation for good food, and the impossibility of getting a table.

'I had my secretary book a table for eight o'clock. We're a little early, but I don't suppose that'll be a problem at this time in the evening.' He climbed from the cab, holding the door for her.

'Look, I know you said we'd have dinner, but honestly I've got a pile of work—'

'India,' he said, cutting her short. And the way he used her given name was faintly shocking. Like being touched. 'I've been chasing you around that wretched store all day. I've been very, very patient, and you will now do me the courtesy of sitting down and sharing a meal with me. I want to hear about your plans. How you see the future of Claibourne & Farraday.'

'In my hands,' she replied, without missing a beat. And the changes she had in mind were not for sharing with Jordan Farraday.

His smile was perfunctory. 'Humour me, as I've humoured you all day, or the shadow deal's off and you can forget all about me playing follow-my-leader for the rest of the month. Instead I'll instruct my lawyers to invoke the golden share agreement first thing tomorrow.'

That wretched 'golden share'... The two per cent controlling interest in the company that was supposed to be handed on, like some Olympic flame, to the oldest male heir. Not this time.

He might be oldest; she was best.

'In which case,' he added, just in case she hadn't got the point, 'you'll be out by the end of the week.'

'You can try,' she said, not moving. 'Once the lawyers get involved it could take years.' Except that would defeat the whole object. She might be in, occupying the seat, but she wouldn't be able to do a thing. Any move to change the name, change the style, do anything constructive, would be met with legal injunctions. The company would stagnate, wither.

She would surrender before she'd let that happen. She just hoped he didn't know that.

'So…' he said. 'We both know exactly where we stand. No more pretending to be nice. You have possession of the store and you'll do anything to keep it. Something that I can't possibly allow.' Then, 'But we still have to eat.' And he offered her his hand.

Damn! She hadn't planned on things moving this quickly. A fact she was sure he knew. He knew altogether too much. All day he'd been at her shoulder, stealing the limelight, charming everyone he met, apparently interested in the smallest detail, always asking the right questions.

Always there, just at the corner of her vision, close enough to touch but never quite touching.

She'd tossed her sisters into this situation without a thought as to how they'd cope. She'd just wanted the time it had bought her. The time it had bought her lawyers as they tried to make a case to stop the takeover.

Faced with the reality of spending a month in this

man's company…up close and as personal as it got…she wished she'd listened to their protests.

She wished they were home, so that she could talk to them. Romana had taken time out from her extended honeymoon to e-mail her detailed ideas for the better use of space—ideas that she'd wasted no time in implementing. And Flora had sent back wonderful cloth, jewellery and design sketches, as well as a report for the travel department on Saraminda.

Neither of them had offered advice on dealing with a Farraday male. Maybe because they knew their solution could never be hers.

She'd never felt so alone in her life.

When she still hesitated, he let his hand drop and said, 'If you doubt that I can do it, I'll tell the driver to take you back to the store. But I suggest you clear your desk while you're there.'

She could scarcely believe her ears. 'You're threatening me?'

'No, India. I don't make threats to get what I want. What I'm doing is giving you a month of my time in which to convince me that you're the only person in the world who can run Claibourne & Farraday.'

'Why?' The word escaped her lips before she could stop it. 'Why are you doing that?'

'Giving you a month of my time?'

'Yes. What's in it for you?'

'Well, let's see. I'm doing it because your lawyers requested it and my lawyers could see no disadvantage. I'm taking the opportunity to familiarise myself with the store. Get to know the senior staff.' She wished she hadn't asked. He was using the time she'd given him to infiltrate himself into the store, smooth the transition… 'What I'm doing is bending over backwards to be reasonable, so that if we do end up in a court battle I'll impress their Lordships as a reasonable man who's done everything asked.' And he smiled. 'Does that answer your question?'

His answer was so smooth, so pat. So…*reasonable*! She couldn't fault him. Which meant she'd just have to swallow her pride and play nice.

'Yes, well, I've never suggested I'm the only person in the world who can run the store, JD,' she said, finally joining him on the pavement. If he was going to make free with *her* name, without so much as a by-you-leave, she certainly wasn't going to keep calling him Mr Farraday. As if he were the boss and she were his underling. They were equals. As he turned from paying the driver, she dredged up a smile. 'Just the best.'

'Jordan,' he said.

'What?'

'My staff call me JD. You and I are equals.' *Equals?* Could he read her mind? 'Partners. I'd rather you called me by my name.' He lifted his brows, encouraging her to give it a try.

'Jordan?' she offered.

He lifted the corner of his mouth in a wry smile. 'That wasn't so difficult, was it?'

Patronising oaf. She didn't believe for one minute that he considered her his equal, but she'd do her level best to change his mind—and if that involved supping with the devil, she'd do it. She put a little more effort into her smile as he placed his hand beneath her elbow—did he feel her jump as he touched her?—pushed open the restaurant door and held it for her.

'It's curious that we're both named after countries, don't you think?' he said, once they were seated at a quiet table.

She resisted the temptation to point out that while he was named after a very small country she was named after a sub-continent. 'My father met my mother in India,' she said, perusing the menu. 'Hence the name. It's something of a family tradition. My father took his second wife to Florence for their honeymoon, and met his third in Rome on a trip to the fashion shows. She was a model. Hence Flora and Romana.'

'How fortunate he didn't have boys.'

She glanced up. 'Well, that's original.'

'What is?'

'Most people say how lucky it was that the cities weren't Naples, or Pisa. Tell me about your name. Was that a honeymoon destination too?'

'My parents never got around to taking a honeymoon,' he replied. 'But then they never actually got around to marriage.'

'Oh.' Served her right for asking.

'According to my mother, my father's surname was Jordan. Or rather Jourdan. He was French. They met while she was backpacking in Europe before going to university. It was one of those holiday romances. You know how it is. Brief. Passionate.' He shrugged. 'Life-changing.'

Was it a big deal having a baby as a single mother back then? She supposed it must have been. Something about the way he'd said 'life-changing' suggested it had radically changed his mother's life. And not necessarily for the better. Not going to university would have been the first of many sacrifices.

'I did wonder how you came to be using the Farraday surname,' she said. She'd resisted the urge to ask. She didn't want to know that kind of stuff. She had to keep this businesslike. 'You never knew him?'

'My father? No. He was long gone by the time Kitty realised she was pregnant.'

'Kitty? You call your mother by her first name?'

He shrugged. 'A gloss to protect my grandfather's sensibilities, I suspect.'

'Oh, I see. I'm sorry. I didn't mean to pry. I just don't know much about your family history.'

'We have a lot in common, you and I. We both want the same thing. We both come from one-parent families.'

She wanted to ask him if his mother had ever found someone special. Wanted to know about his life. Had he been an only child? The son of an embittered woman? An older half-sibling... An outsider... This morning he had been a stranger. Already she wanted to know his deepest fears, his happiest memories.

'She gave you his name,' she said.

'Not the whole name. But she felt I should have something to remember him by. The way your name reminds you of your mother. Do you remember her?'

'No. I was still a baby when she left.' So much for keeping it businesslike. Concentrating on the menu, as if she hadn't already made up her mind what she would choose, and as casually as she knew how, she said, 'According to my grandmother she never settled—hated London. She just wanted to go back to India, kick off her shoes, don her beads and get back to the ashram.'

'Without you.' Without her. She was twenty-nine years old, quite old enough to understand that not all women were natural mothers, but her casual abandonment still had the power to hurt. 'What did your father say?' he asked.

'Not much. Just that things had probably turned out for the best. But then I'm sure you already knew that, since it was apparently covered comprehensively in the gossip columns at the time.'

'You haven't read the cuttings?'

'Would you?' She shrugged. 'Opinion seems to have been that I was better off in a well-organised nursery with a nanny who knew what she was doing.'

'And your mother agreed to that? Your father just let her go? They hadn't been married more than a few weeks.'

'Are you asking me to justify his decision? Or explain the actions of a woman I haven't seen since I was three months old?'

'You must have thought about it.'

'Of course. But my father was struggling to come to grips with taking over Claibourne & Farraday after your grandfather's death. He wasn't in any position to chase after her.' The easy answers flowed from her lips, as they had flowed from her grandmother's whenever she'd asked about the exotically lovely girl in the photographs who was, apparently, her mother. Then, as if it didn't matter to her, 'And you know my father: the man who invented the trophy wife. It must have been a complete mismatch. The surprising thing is that they ever got around to marriage, considering how much my grandmother disapproved of her.' But then her grandmother was a bigot and snob. 'You obviously know that it was something of a last-minute affair.'

'A quick trip to the register office on the way to the delivery room is the way I heard it. But then I imagine he was aware that with a wedding he'd have had a stronger claim on you.' She glanced up from the menu. 'Your mother could have taken you back to India with her and disapeared,' he explained. 'He might have a short attention span when it comes to women, but your father has made a point of keeping his children close.'

India had never seen it that way. When you only ever heard one side of the story… She swallowed, then, as if it was of no interest to her either way, 'I think you probably got it right the first time, Jordan. I think my grandmother is the one who made a point of holding his family fast. I'll have the roast sea bream,' she said, discarding the menu. 'You seem very well informed about my family.'

'The Claibournes are our partners. Naturally I'm interested in everything you do. Surely you've got files on us?'

'To be honest, I've never actually thought that much about the Farradays,' she said dismissively.

'A mistake.'

'Evidently. But honestly I didn't think you cared. You're just the "and" part of the name. Totally uninterested in the store.'

'Oh, come on. You can't believe that.' He frowned. 'Do you?'

'We've never even met before today,' she reminded him. 'I didn't know about the golden share until the lawyers told me about it.'

'Your father never warned you?'

'I imagine he thought I'd be safely married with other things to keep me busy by the time he retired. Unfortunately the heart attack brought things forward.'

He regarded her with those unreadable eyes. 'No plans in that direction?'

'Marriage?' He shrugged, suggesting that it wasn't the only option these days. 'Who has the time?' she said. 'With my father's example, who'd have the inclination? You?' she asked.

'Work seems to take up all my time.' After what seemed an age, he turned to the waiter and gave their order. 'Something to drink, India?'

'Mineral water. Still. No ice or lemon.'

There was a moment of silence. 'My secretary suggested I propose a dynastic marriage,' Jordan said after a while. 'To settle all arguments. For ever.'

India cleared her throat. 'Isn't that a little presumptuous? For a secretary?'

'Maybe. But Christine will tell you herself, without shame, that she's the best secretary in the world.' His smile suggested that he agreed with her.

'Even so.'

'She was taking the pragmatic view. What she had in mind was a kind of…well, merger,' he said, his voice lingering over 'merger', the soft burr in his voice suggesting a lot more than an alliance of business partners, tugging at some soft core inside her, making her feel very conscious of his masculinity. 'The kind that was once commonplace. To unite fortunes, great estates—'

'Department stores?' Her ripple of laughter suggested that he could not possibly be serious. 'Oh, please.'

'I believe the picture of Flora and Bram's wedding in some gossip magazine put the idea into her head,' he continued. Seriously.

Serious, he was even more dangerous than when he was smiling. The smile could be discounted as window dressing, but serious…

She floundered for a moment as a fighter squadron of butterflies attacked her stomach. He couldn't… He wouldn't…

'Sally…my secretary…showed me the photograph too. She didn't suggest we follow suit, however. Clearly,' she suggested, 'my secretary is brighter than your secretary.'

'Sally's a charming girl.'

'With a live-in boyfriend who plays prop forward for the London Irish,' she said. Then wished she hadn't. Before he could respond, she picked up her handbag and took out the weekly event schedule for the store, which was tucked into her diary. 'Now, tomorrow—'

He reached out and grasped her wrist, stopping her before she could begin. 'Tomorrow,' he said, 'before we do anything else, I want you to show me exactly what you're doing to the top floor.'

His fingers were long and strong, dark against the paler skin of her wrist, and his touch tingled like an electric shock. 'You're supposed to be shadowing me, Jordan,' she said, concentrating very hard on keeping her breathing even, light. 'Observing what I do. Not dictating my timetable.' She wanted to snatch her hand back, rub away the pressure of her fingers against her skin, blink and break eye contact. But she did none of those things. Instead she tried to think of something very, very dull while she kept her gaze fixed on the bridge of his nose. It was an old trick one of her nannies had taught her, to outstare some girl who'd been giving her a hard time at school. It never failed.

This time she thought it might, but then, without warning, he released her wrist and sat back as the waiter appeared with their drinks. 'Frankly,' he said, 'I'd be a little more impressed if you were doing your own job, instead of rushing around standing in for Romana, doing the PR stuff that she would normally be taking care of.'

So. He'd noticed that she wasn't sticking to her usual routine. 'You're getting two for the price of one this month. Managing Director and PR Director. Of course it wouldn't be necessary if your cousin hadn't persuaded her to run away with him and...*merge*,' she retaliated.

'You know that's what happened for a fact, do you?' he enquired. 'You don't think it might have been the other way around?'

Which suggested he was as much in the dark about it as she was. 'Are you telling me that he hasn't called in? Made his report?' She smiled, as if she knew the whole story, then, since she knew no more than he did, moved swiftly on before he could uncover her own uncertainties. 'I was about to say that first thing tomorrow morning I have a meeting with the surveyor to check on the progress of the alterations, if you'd like to join me. It's at eight o'clock.'

'I'll be there,' he said, then gave the waiter their order. When the man had gone, he sat back. 'What do you do when you're not working?'

'I'm sorry? I thought the purpose of eating together was so that I could brief you on what will be happening at Claibourne's this month. And my plans for the store.'

'Claibourne & Farraday. The store has two names,' he reminded her. 'Other people may refer to the store as Claibourne's for convenience, or out of laziness. You should never dilute your own brand image.'

About to say that Claibourne's *was* the brand image these days, she thought better of it. He was quite sharp enough to pick up the smallest clues from her voice without her putting up a target and inviting him to shoot it down. 'Shall we get on? An hour isn't long to explain what we're doing. Less.' She glanced at her wristwatch. 'Fifty-two minutes.'

'Leave it. I picked up a copy of the store programme for the next week. As for the alterations, that'll be simpler if we go through it tomorrow, when we're with the surveyor.'

'That's just the practical stuff. Aren't you interested in my vision for the future?' she asked.

'I could probably tell you now, word for word, what you're going to say. Expansion, modernisation, ordering online—'

'That's already in place.'

'And yet you give the impression of being such a delightfully old-fashioned emporium.'

'Only the service is old-fashioned.'

'And the style of the store. You really should get those carpets ripped out. They're very…yesterday.'

'They're *what*?'

'Yesterday. It's an expression much used by the interior designer who's working on my offices at the moment.'

'I see. Well, yes, he's right. Polished floors are back in vogue, and much more in keeping with the arts and crafts interiors. The carpets are history.'

'She.'

'What?'

'The interior designer is a woman. From the attention I'm getting I imagine she's hoping I'll let her loose on Claibourne & Farraday. When I take over.' India was immediately assailed with a vision of some incredibly elegant young woman, tempting Jordan Farraday with exotic wood floors and anything else that took his fancy in return for the opportunity to remodel Claibourne's. She gave herself a mental shaking. In return for nothing. Forget Claibourne's. He wouldn't have to offer inducements to have women wanting to be nice. He'd just have to lift the corner of his mouth in that come-and-get-me smile and he'd be fighting them off...

'You won't need a designer. The arts and crafts interiors are listed, as is the stained glass. They can't be touched. And the original wood floors are still there, beneath the carpets, just waiting to be sanded, polished and sealed.'

'I know that. She doesn't. It's keeping her very keen.' And he used that smile on her. She might be a woman famously hard to impress, but hormones that had lain undisturbed for what seemed like years were suddenly wide awake and panting eagerly. 'But I've had enough shop talk for tonight. Right now, India, I'm more interested in you. What you do with your spare time?'

She swallowed. Reminded herself that this was business and that what she did with her spare time was none of his. 'That...Jordan...is none of your business,' she said firmly.

'I know.' He sat forward. 'That's what makes it so interesting.'

'Maybe so, but I think we should keep this on a purely business footing.'

Undeterred, he said, 'I have press cuttings of you going back years—'

'Years? How many years?'

'I believe you were four years old on the first occasion you were trotted out for a publicity shot. And very sweet you looked, sitting on Santa's knee.'

Oh, good grief. 'You raided the newspaper archives for *that*?'

'It wasn't necessary. A cuttings agency have kept us up to date. You may not find us that interesting, but we find the Claibournes endlessly fascinating. Your father's many marriages and affairs have never left us short of something sensational to read. However, there's nothing—beyond the usual youthful nonsense—to suggest that you have much of a personal life these days. Not recently anyway.'

'Not one that would interest the gossip columns,' she admitted. 'I'm much too busy for such nonsense.'

'You must do something other than empire-build.'

India had thought she'd done her research on Jordan Farraday and his cousins. She'd needed to know what kind of men she was dealing with. But she'd confined her enquiries to the recent past. Their careers, their ambitions. She couldn't compete with a lifetime's obsession.

'Must I?' she asked. 'What do *you* do in *your* spare time?'

'I asked first,' he pointed out. And he sat back in his chair and regarded her for a moment. When she didn't volunteer an answer, he probed further. 'Do you go to the theatre?'

'The store sponsored a charity gala a couple of months ago. Your cousin Niall was there. It was the day he began shadowing Romana,' she said. It was scarcely subtle as a reminder of what had happened to Niall Farraday Macaulay when *he'd* stopped talking shop.

Jordan acknowledged her response with the slightest lift of his brows, but didn't pursue it. 'Do you enjoy sports?' He seemed determined to uncover her private life.

'We sponsored a pro-am golf tournament last year,' she replied coolly, equally determined to keep the conversation on a purely business level, confident that she could keep this up all night. 'I presented the prizes. Does that count?' she asked, picking up her glass and filling her mouth with ice-cold water.

'What about sex? Do you manage to find time for that?' The water exploded down her nose. Jordan calmly handed her a handkerchief. 'Or do you sponsor someone else to do that while you watch too?'

'Bastard,' she said, then as she blew her nose realised what she'd said and groaned. But when she finally emerged from behind the handkerchief he was laughing.

'I do believe we're getting somewhere at last,' he said.

'I'm sorry… I didn't mean…'

He raised his hand to stop her apology. 'Please… It was worth it to see you blush.'

'Blush? Oh, come on. I don't blush.'

'Of course you don't.' And he did that thing with his eyebrows again. The you-should-be-where-I'm-sitting thing. He did have the most amazingly expressive eyebrows.

'And the answer to your question is no,' she finished.

'No time? Or no, you don't sponsor someone else to do it for you?'

This time the blush was undeniably fierce enough to heat her cheeks, but she wasn't going to allow him to win this round on points. 'It's been three years, two months and six days.' That fixed the eyebrows. 'In answer to the "Do I have time?" question. He was the most charming man. We'd known one another for years. But three years, two months and six days ago he asked me to marry him.'

'That would have been James Cawston.' He hadn't been kidding about the cuttings agency. James had squired her about the place for a long time, and it was inevitable that they would have been photographed together, their relationship noted, speculated upon. 'And obviously you said no.'

'Not as such. I'd just been made a director of the store and I had other things on my mind. When I asked him to wait he said he wouldn't waste his time since it was clear that I was already married to the store.' When Jordan didn't comment, she risked another, careful sip of water. 'Well?' she asked, finally unnerved by his thoughtful expression. His apparently endless silence as he considered what she'd told him indicated that he was clearly reading far more into her revelation than she'd ever intended. She'd enjoyed James's friendship, had missed him being there whenever she'd needed a man at her side. But the fact that she'd let him walk away without doing a thing to prevent it had left her in no doubt that he'd been right. Maybe she was more like her father than she'd like to admit. Forced to choose between her mother and the store, he'd chosen the store—and he was nowhere near as passionate about it as she was. 'Was that interesting enough for you?'

'Three years, two months and six days?'

She realised that her precision had suggested she was brooding about it, heartbroken. 'I don't get that many marriage proposals,' she said. 'The date is fixed in my mind. You'll notice I wasn't counting the hours and minutes.'

'Are you suggesting it wasn't that serious?'

'Not for me. But it occurred to me that James was probably right, and I didn't want anyone else to be as hurt as he obviously was at the time. Hence the lack of a social life these days.'

'Three years is a long time. Too long.'

'Really? Are you speaking from personal experience, here?' He didn't leap to answer, and, because she'd said more than enough about her personal life, she turned the spotlight on him. 'What about you, Jordan?'

'What about me?'

'What do you do when you aren't busy making money? Are you a supporter of the arts? Do you enjoy sport?' She raised her hand in a gesture that invited him to fill the gaps. Then, after an epic pause, 'And what about sex?' she added.

'What about it?'

'Are you a participant or a spectator?'

CHAPTER FOUR

INDIA instantly wished the words unsaid. Jordan had been tempting her along this path for the last ten minutes or so. First he'd turned the conversation to her family and then he'd concentrated on her, drawing her out, probing her defences with sympathy, with humour, with such skill that she'd forgotten all about sticking to business. Keeping it impersonal. And stepped right off the cliff edge.

Now she had two choices. Opt for safety: laugh, change the subject. And give him the satisfaction of knowing that he'd caught her out. Won. Or take him over the edge with her.

There was no contest.

'Well?' she prompted, raising her eyebrows, inviting Jordan to lay his own life bare. 'I occasionally get to the theatre,' he admitted. 'Or a concert. Not as often as I'd like.'

'Why?' He hadn't been reserved about asking her questions, after all. She was certainly entitled to know everything about the man who intended to take her life's work away from her.

'Finding the time, a companion with similar tastes...' He shrugged. 'I can't stand twittering women.'

Serious theatre, serious music, then. And she felt a certain empathy with his plight. 'I feel just the same way about twittering men,' she assured him, but crisply. She didn't want the fellow feeling to show. 'The ones who will insist on telling you about the tough day they've had at the Stock Exchange while all you want is a quiet moment to contemplate the incredible performance you've just heard.'

He greeted this with a half smile of recognition. 'And yet without someone to share the pleasure…' He left the sentiment unfinished, as if inviting her to agree with him, and his words found an answering echo in her own life. She understood the emptiness, the need to reach out for the hand of someone who understood exactly what you were feeling without the need for words.

She'd tried going to concerts on her own but it had seemed a hollow experience.

Her mind, though, was swift to fill in a picture of the same experience shared with Jordan Farraday, and she found herself wishing he were not the enemy. So powerful was the image that she caught her lower lip between her teeth, as if to prevent the words from spilling out.

There was too much common ground between them already. They both wanted the same thing. But she was going to have to work ten times as hard as he was to get it.

When she didn't respond, take the lead he'd offered, he let it go.

'As for sport,' he went on, 'I play cricket for a City team a couple of times a year. Does that count?'

'Twice a year? Oh, that's serious,' she said, gently mocking him as she grabbed at the opportunity to retreat from the sudden searing intensity of discovering shared feelings, the same empty spaces in their busy lives.

'Deadly serious,' he assured her, and despite her teasing she didn't doubt it. She thought that he probably did everything that way. Except smile. His smile was a lazy thing. It started at the right-hand corner of his mouth and rarely got much further. But that was far enough for most purposes. More than enough to make a woman want to smile back. 'We only play a couple of matches a year, but we play to win.' Then, the smile deepening slightly, 'The losers buy drinks on the house at the local hostelry all Saturday night.'

'Oh, I see. It's just a serious excuse for a party.'

'It's a weekend in the country. A chance to get together outside of the City and let off a little steam. No shop talk allowed. And we raise money for charity, too, although we don't use it as a PR exercise to advertise ourselves,' he added. An insult so subtle that it took a moment to sink in. At which point she wished she hadn't been so fast to respond to that smile. He waited to see if she had anything more to say on the subject, then, 'We're playing this weekend, as a matter of fact. I thought that for once I might have to give it a miss because of work-shadowing you.'

'Weekends would become a thing of the past if—' She stopped. Even to suggest that he might win was to tempt fate.

'Then I shall make the most of it while I have the opportunity. Maybe you'd like to come along?'

'And shadow you instead?' She gave a little shrug. 'Why would I want to do that?'

'A small courtesy in return for all the time I'm giving you?'

'I thought having dinner with you was compensating for that. And you really don't have to stick to me through every working hour.' She tucked her hair behind her ear, offering him a smile of her own. The cool, you're-not-getting-away-with-this smile. 'You were quick enough to make your excuses and leave this morning, when my celebrity author fixed you in her sights. She wasn't deterred by your swift departure, by the way. She phoned and left a message with Sally inviting you to dinner. Sally made your excuses, said you had a business dinner—'

'She's got a great future ahead of her.'

'She had no idea it was true. So I'm repaying you twice.' He didn't deny it. 'You can take the weekend off just as easily. Go and have fun with your friends. I won't tell.'

'Who is there to tell?' he asked. And he reached out, took her hand, held it between his. 'This is between the two of us, India.' There was an intensity about his expression, the slow precision of his words. 'No one else.' For a moment she thought he was talking about more than the store. Then the corner of his mouth lifted a fraction higher, acknowledging the fact that she'd love to have him out of her hair for a couple of days. 'I've dedicated this month one hundred per cent to Claibourne & Farraday and to you. Where you go, I go.' Her hand in his suggested that was the way it would always be. 'Do you have any plans for this weekend?' he asked.

She blinked, and suddenly the moment was over. She retrieved her hand. 'Other than work?' she asked. 'Nothing exciting.' Far from it. This weekend was dedicated to reading and re-reading through those old files Sally had found. There might be something that would help her. Something to explain why her father had never told her about the golden share. She wasn't about to tell Jordan

Farraday that. 'Nothing that you'd have to stay in London for,' she assured him instead. 'And it would be unkind to make you miss your rare sporting weekend.'

'Does that mean you'll come?'

Of course it didn't. It meant he could go. Without her.

She envied him. It was months since she'd had even a day off. Maybe that was part of the problem. She was stale, her mind fogged with the endless meetings with lawyers. Quite unable to switch off, forget it even in her sleep.

A little fresh air in a work-free zone might be just what she needed to give her a fresh perspective on her problems. But not with Jordan Farraday tagging along as a constant reminder of the ticking clock.

'It doesn't mean anything of the sort. I said that you could go. What would I do at a cricket match?'

'Make the tea?'

'Very funny.' She tried to read his face, feel what he was thinking, but he was giving nothing away. Not a man to second-guess or play poker with—always supposing she knew how.

He shrugged. 'It's your choice.'

'Just like it was my choice to have dinner with you?'

'If my company is that onerous,' he replied, his voice as expressionless as his face, 'you could surrender the store right now and save yourself a month of misery.'

Surrender? A tremor of alarm swept through her. Was he that confident? 'Dream on,' she said, doing her level best to match his lack of emotion.

'Your decision. The Farradays are a patient lot. We've waited thirty years. We can wait another four weeks.' Thirty years? She caught a glimmer of something... 'But

I'll be sorry if you decide not to join us,' he said, distracting her.

He wanted her company? 'Why?' she asked carelessly. Then worked it out for herself. 'Oh, of course. The tea. Twenty-two men can eat a lot of sandwiches.'

'Sandwiches,' he confirmed. 'Cakes. Scones. How are your scones?'

'Of all the chauvinist, sexist things I've ever heard—' She was, unusually, lost for words. Nothing, but nothing, would induce her to spend a weekend slaving over a breadboard while the men were, well…being men.

And yet her curiosity was piqued. What was Jordan Farraday really like behind the cool smile and the uniform of the City? Chalk-stripe suit, white linen shirt and a tie that would open any door. It looked good on him, very good, and if he lingered for any length of time in the menswear department sales of that particular combination would soar, she knew. But it was still a uniform of a kind. Shorthand for everything he represented.

In the country, relaxing with friends, his guard down, she'd learn far more about him than he'd ever reveal while he was wearing that suit. She'd never have a better chance to get to know the man. Or find out what he really wanted. Because she wasn't convinced that he saw himself stepping into her father's shoes.

Enigmatic, distant, never fodder for gossip columnists, the man was practically invisible. The one indisputable fact that her researchers had uncovered about him was that running a department store—even a store with the cachet of Claibourne & Farraday—would be very small beer to JD Farraday.

She realised that he was waiting, brows slightly raised,

for her to complete her tirade regarding the exploitative nature of the male.

She just knew he had some slick phrase ready to make her appear foolish. 'I thought you said your cricket weekends were a work-free zone,' she said.

He shrugged. 'We all leave our laptops and our mobile phones at home. Even the women,' he added—a touch mockingly, she thought. 'But we still have to eat.'

'Twenty-two hungry men?'

'Twenty-four. Don't forget the umpires.'

'Heaven forbid.' Then, 'Oh, I get it. You're all expected to take along a woman to pitch in and do the chores while you're having fun—someone to peel the potatoes and make sure you don't starve. And you're fresh out of women.'

Except she couldn't believe that. He'd never be short of a woman to wash his socks. Or make his sandwiches. Someone tall and slender and blonde…

'Not necessarily a woman,' he said, interrupting her train of thought—something he was remarkably good at. 'We have no fixed ideas regarding gender roles. One of our batsmen is a woman. Her husband makes the best bacon sandwiches in the world.' He held his finger and thumb a couple of inches apart. 'This thick.'

'Yummy,' she replied unenthusiastically, trying not to look at his long fingers, the way his thumb curved… 'I'm afraid,' she said, feeling suddenly rather warm and sitting back in her chair, putting the maximum distance between them, 'that baking really isn't my thing. In fact my rock cakes are indistinguishable from builders' rubble.' She lifted her shoulders a millimetre. 'Sorry.' Then, 'If you're short of a partner why don't you invite your interior designer along? I'm sure she'll make incredibly elegant sandwiches, with the fillings co-ordinated to match your team colours.' *Oh, miaow!* She couldn't believe how catty that sounded. 'I'm sure she'd be delighted to don a pinny and pitch in. She's got more to gain than I have.'

'She might think that. She'd be wrong.' And he smiled again. She wished he wouldn't do that! 'While *you* have the fate of an entire department store hanging in the balance.'

Jordan watched India's expression as she battled with an urgent desire to fling her glass of water over him.

That he deserved it, glass and all, he didn't doubt. It was a pity. Inviting her to spend the weekend with him had come out of nowhere. It hadn't been planned, which bothered him slightly. He didn't do spur of the moment. Not when it was this important.

If he'd planned it he'd have made rather more effort to make sure she said yes. Presented it as an opportunity for her to pitch her case. Offered her some personal advantage in accepting.

His timing had been way off…but then it had been that kind of day. He'd been doing the right thing, saying the right thing, but he wasn't getting the responses he expected. It was as if ever since that girl went into labour the world had been slightly out of kilter.

Or maybe it was from the moment he'd looked up and realised India Claibourne was a lot more than a beautiful face.

He'd anticipated a pampered woman, living off her name, running the store as hobby while someone else did all the hard work. Just as her father had done. A day spent at her shoulder, watching her at work, had given him the unsettling feeling that she was the one her father had left the hard work to in recent years.

Not that she made it look that way.

There was an effortless ease in the way she covered the ground, handled queries, got things done. He knew just how much real effort that took out of hours, after business was done for the day. How much background knowledge was needed to make decisions—the right decisions—on the move. He understood that kind of effort.

He'd thought he understood India Claibourne. He'd done his homework, studied her form. It was easy to admire her for her looks, her style. It came as something of a shock to realise that he admired her for her brain.

Not that cleverness would help her. His intention to evict India Claibourne and her sisters from the boardroom of Claibourne & Farraday, claim it for his own, was fixed, immutable. And the cleverer she was, the greater the triumph.

Yet he couldn't help wishing he'd handled his invitation to join him for weekend with a little more finesse. It might have been thrown out on the spur of the moment, but on this occasion, he suspected, impulse knew better than intellect.

The glass of water remained untouched on the table and she kept very still, presumably while she counted to ten. Then, as if she'd made up her mind about something, she once more reached for the silky dark curtain of hair that brushed her cheek—a giveaway gesture, though quite what it was giving away he hadn't decided—and hooked it behind her ear.

'Where do you stay?' she asked. The question was so

unexpected that it took him a moment to organise a coherent answer. Was she offering him a second chance to tempt her? And if so, why? 'During this sporting excuse for overeating?'

He brain freewheeled for a moment. 'One of our members has a country house with its own cricket pitch.' He ignored the odd little heartleap at the thought of spending a weekend in her company, away from the mahogany splendour of Claibourne & Farraday. All day he'd been conscious of her hair shining at his eyeline, swinging, sliding silkily as she turned to look up at him. Conscious of the subtle scent she wore. The way she moved…

'That sounds rather grand.'

He forced himself, instead, to ponder what advantage she'd perceived in taking up his invitation. There had to be one. 'It's very informal,' he assured her.

'No suits, no highheels, no mobile phones for two whole days? It sounds almost irresistible.'

Her mind was made up, he realised, torn between wariness and triumph. She was going to come. She was simply going through the motions of allowing herself to be talked into it. 'There are fines for anyone caught using a phone of any description,' he said.

'Oh, that's harsh.'

'It's one way of raising money for the good cause nominated for the weekend.'

She smiled. 'You mean they all subscribe to the theory, but the reality is more than they can cope with?'

'Something like that.'

'I haven't had a break in months. Even with the prospect of buttering endless slices of bread, it is tempting.'

Was that it? Could it be that she was simply tempted by the prospect of a weekend in the country?

With the enemy? How likely was that? She could undoubtedly call on any number of friends who'd be happy to entertain her.

And yet the prospect of continuing this verbal fencing match in more relaxed surroundings was unexpectedly exciting.

'Is that a step up from "maybe" to "definite"?' he asked.

'It's a step up to definitely...' her lashes swept down, disguising her thoughts '...maybe.' No—it wasn't likely at all. This was purely business. She had no intention of relaxing—whatever she might say—and neither would he. 'No business?' she pressed, as if mocking him.

'Absolutely none,' he replied. 'And it isn't all catering, I promise. There is a staff. But with so many of us...' He left her imagination to fill in the blank. 'There's a heated outdoor pool for those who get bored lying in a deckchair watching the game.'

'Oh, now I'm seriously tempted,' she said. 'How soon would you have to know?'

'I'll have a bag in my car on Friday. If you want to come, just show up in the car park at six.'

'And if I don't?'

He felt an overwhelming urge to push her into coming with him. 'Then we'll both spend a summer weekend in London, shut in an office going through the financial statements for the last year along with your sales projections for the coming year,' he said, offering her a vision of hell. 'Both of us wishing we were sitting in a country meadow eating asparagus and strawberries fresh from the kitchen garden.'

'The asparagus might just be the clincher,' she admitted, with an unforced smile that lit up her face in a manner that revealed the professional business smile for what it was—genuine enough, and a pleasure in itself, but with a touch of reserve that was missing from the real thing. Then, as their food arrived, 'I'll see how the week develops and let you know.'

He knew better than to push for a decision, and as they gave their full attention to their meal he steered the conversation to safely neutral ground. A recent art exhibition. An Oscar Wilde revival they'd both seen. Finding common ground. Touching minds. Discovering that they had a lot more than a department store in common.

But they didn't linger, declining dessert and coffee and by mutual consent walking the short distance back to the Claibourne & Farraday car park, passing the silent store with its exquisite window displays.

At the main entrance she paused and glanced up at the two names, side by side. 'They've been there a long time. It seems extraordinary that we've never met before,' India said, after a moment.

He turned to look down at her. 'Maybe you should ask your father the reason for that.'

'Dad?' Her face was lit up by the window displays and he saw the frown creasing the wide space between her brows. 'Why? What's it got to do with him?'

She hadn't a clue, he realised. Had no idea about her father's role in what had happened thirty years earlier. 'That's for him to tell you, not me.'

'He's away. Convalescing after his heart attack. You know that.'

'So I heard.' The man hadn't had the courage to tell her that she didn't stand a chance of hanging onto the store. Or did he hope—head in the sand—that by removing himself from the scene he would defuse the situation? That the Farradays would leave India and her sisters to run things undisturbed? Surely he couldn't be that naïve? 'Come on. I'll see you to your car.'

For a moment she looked as if she might dig her heels in, demand to know everything that he knew. Maybe something in his expression warned her that it was a waste of time. Or maybe it was just the suggestion that she needed a man to walk her down a quiet side street in the middle of London at any time of the day or night that turned those warm brown eyes to stone.

Whatever the reason, she spun on her heel and without another word headed for the car park at the rear of the store so fast that he was forced to lengthen his stride to keep up with her.

'India—' he began, not knowing exactly what he intended to say, only that he didn't want to end the day on a sour note.

'I'll see you in the morning, Jordan,' she said briskly, not looking back as she approached her Mercedes coupé, unlocking the door with the remote control on her key-ring.

'For the meeting with the surveyor at eight o'clock,' he said, bending swiftly to open it for her, holding it as she slid behind the driving wheel and started the engine. 'I'll be here,' he said, closing the door and then taking a sharp step backwards to avoid her car as she swung it out of the parking space and accelerated towards the ramp in a manner that suggested she was not entirely enthusiastic about the idea.

He remained where he was for a moment, angry with himself for putting her on the defensive—that had been careless—and disturbed by an unfamiliar feeling of regret.

'Was that Miss India?' He turned as a security guard materialised at his side, a little short of breath and clutching a small cardboard box. 'She normally comes into the security office before she goes.'

'She was in something of a hurry…Gareth,' he said, glancing at the man's security badge. 'Can I help? I'm Jordan Farraday,' he added, when the man looked doubtful. 'You'll have seen the name above the door.'

'Sorry, sir, I didn't recognise you.'

'There's no reason why you should. What's the problem?'

'Well, it's these.' He held out the box for Jordan to check the contents. And if he'd ever believed in Santa Claus he'd have thought it was Christmas.

India pulled into her parking space at the riverside apartment block she called home. For a moment she just sat there, her hands wrapped tightly about the steering wheel.

What on earth was going on? What did her father know about the dispute with the Farradays? He'd kept the golden share from her. What else hadn't he told her?

What did Jordan know that she didn't? Why his resentment of the Claibournes? There had been no Farraday heir thirty years ago.

Even now Jordan didn't want the store. What he wanted was control of the assets. The final say when it came to making the big decisions. And the biggest decision was whether to sell out to one of the major retail groups.

Her father had had offers, she knew. He might have been a very average businessman, less interested in Claibourne & Farraday than in the glamorous young women who shopped there. But at least he hadn't taken the easy option and sold out to the highest bidder. Would Jordan do that?

She stirred. She wouldn't find any answers sitting behind the wheel of her car, and she took the box of old files from the boot and carried them up to her apartment.

Once there, she showered and changed into a pair of jogging pants and a T-shirt, soft with washing and as comfortable as an old slipper. Then she curled up on the sofa, nursing a mug of tea between her hands, and stared at the files. Willing them to contain something that would clear up all the unanswered questions. Putting off the moment when she'd have to look at them, suddenly afraid that they would only make things worse.

It wasn't like her. She dealt with problems head-on. No shilly-shallying. No beating about the bush. But this one was different.

Or maybe it was simply the edgy day she'd had. That constant feeling of being on trial, her every move under the microscope of Jordan Farraday's dark, critical gaze.

And the rather odd evening they'd spent together hadn't helped.

One minute they'd been baiting each other, so that she'd wanted to tell him to do his worst and walk out of the restaurant. The next she'd been offered a tantalising glimpse of something so like perfect harmony that it seemed all she had to do was put out her hand, take his, and say, *This is crazy. We're partners. We should be working together, not fighting each other.*

Crazy, indeed.

She smothered a yawn. She was tired, a little confused, and for the first time since the letter from Jordan Farraday's lawyer had landed on her desk, turning her life upside down, she actually considered the reality of losing the store. The possibility that all her plans might come to nothing. That she'd have to stand back—as the Farradays had done for thirty years—and watch helplessly as Jordan took control.

But she had never run away from anything in her life and this wasn't the time to start. She put down the cup and reached for a file.

As her fingers closed around it there was a long peal on the doorbell.

CHAPTER FIVE

INDIA, her hand stretched out to take the folder, froze momentarily. Then, with a guilty feeling of relief at the interruption, she uncurled herself from the sofa and went to answer the door.

'Okay, what is it this time, George? Coffee, milk…?' she began as she flung it open. Her voice dried on 'bread'. It was not her neighbour, with his forgive-me smile, but the mouth-drying presence of Jordan Farraday that filled her doorway.

She experienced a reprise of that take-your-breath-away moment, a rerun of the instant she'd set eyes on him that morning, as his unexpected appearance on her doorstep left her momentarily bereft of words.

And this time there was no interruption to give her breathing space, no moment of grace in which to recover her wits—or her poise. Just shocked silence as his gaze was momentarily transfixed at the sight of her hair—caught up in a band to keep it from her face—before it swept down over her T-shirt, taking in the shapeless jogging pants before coming to rest on her bare feet.

And then he smiled.

Oh, great.

Here she was, determined that he should be left in no doubt that she was a top-flight business woman, capable of controlling a multi-million-pound retail empire without disturbing a hair of her immaculately coiffured head, and on Day One he'd caught her without the protective armour of her 'image'. Without a scrap of make-up, her hair caught up in a childish hairband that a ten-year-old wouldn't have worn out in daylight, and, as if that wasn't bad enough, wearing her oldest, most cherished, 'comfort' clothes.

He, of course, still looked as a crisply immaculate as he had when she'd first set eyes on him twelve hours earlier. She sweated blood to maintain a public image of unruffled perfection. He clearly achieved this desirable state without raising so much as one of those expressive eyebrows.

'India—'

'Jordan?'

'I'm sorry to disturb you so late.' He didn't look one bit sorry. She wasn't fooled for a minute by that touch of regret in his voice, the conversion of his smile to an expression of remorse at having disturbed her at all. 'Unfortunately, this wouldn't wait.'

What? What wouldn't wait?

And what was in the rather scruffy cardboard box—so at odds with his perfectly groomed appearance—that was balanced between his hands?

She refused to be tempted into asking him, studiously ignored it, instead concentrating on her immediate concern.

'How on earth did you get in?' she demanded. The ring had come at her own door, not at the main entrance to the block, where a high-tech video entry security system was designed to keep unwanted callers—and arrogant tycoons were very high on her list of unwanted callers—out of the building.

'I'm glad you brought that up. I was going to mention the laxity of your security,' he said, taking advantage of her surprise, and the wide open door, to walk right in. And then, when he was on the same side of the door as she was, he turned and said, 'Someone was going out as I arrived and, realising I didn't have a hand free, she held the door for me. Charming woman. Very kind.' He paused, but she wasn't fooled. She knew he hadn't finished. 'And very stupid.'

'Very,' she agreed, although she was quite sure that even the most formidable of women transformed themselves into 'charming', 'kind' and as 'stupid' as it got around Jordan Farraday.

Most women would consider an encounter with him not as a threat—not to their career, at any rate—but as a treat.

She wasn't totally immune to the Farraday effect herself. While the rational part of her struggled to deal with the sensory overload of coming unexpectedly face to face with him in this way, everything feminine in her soul yearned towards him waving frantically and calling, *Me...me...*

Maybe that was why she felt the need to hang onto the door. To stop herself toppling over into his arms.

She had to say something sensible. Let him know that her head wasn't as pleased to see him as the rest of her. 'How did you get my address?' She held up a hand. 'Forget that question. You've got files on me going back to my babyhood, so of course you have my address on file. All you had to do was look it up.'

'Not even that,' he confessed. 'I have a retentive memory.' His mouth tilted in that lazy smile of his. That tugged at every female cell in her body, making her feel wholly, utterly female, undermining all the sensible, level-headed ones warning her that his appearance at her door meant nothing but trouble. 'If you feel at a disadvantage I'll tell you mine,' he offered. And a rerun of the smile made it sound like a variation of that old 'I'll show you mine…' game.

For a moment her lips let her down as they softened into a smile.

No! She snapped them back into line. 'This is a nine-to-five relationship,' she reminded him, ignoring the fact that he was standing in her hall at way past ten o'clock. 'Your office address is all I need.' She found herself wondering what his home was like. Her mind was quick to provide the answer. Something smart. Something expensive. Something very, very classy. Then, since her cool reception hadn't discouraged him, she closed the door. 'What won't keep until tomorrow?'

He didn't seem in any rush to explain himself. Instead he walked through into her living room, setting the box on the low table in front of the sofa. Right next to the files—worn, tatty and spotlit by a tall table lamp that was the only lighting in the room. She clicked on the up-lighters that washed the walls with soft light. Still the files seemed to stand out like a sore thumb against the minimalist perfection of her home.

He couldn't have missed them, but he made no comment. Instead he looked about him, taking in the pale walls, starkly simple furniture, the huge expanse of polished wood flooring. It was a room bereft of fussy detail or clutter. Even her flowers, tall dark blue irises in a straight-sided glass vase, were an exclamation point of colour.

'This is lovely.'

'Claibourne & Farraday Interiors,' she said. 'Not cheap, but very, very good. Try them next time you're decorating.' Then, 'No, sorry, I forgot—you have your own interior designer.'

'At the end of the month Claibourne & Farraday Interiors will be my designers too,' he said. 'In the possessive rather than the client/consultant sense of the word.' Then, turning to face her, 'Who's George?' Had he followed her home simply to remind her that her time was running out? Still reeling from the nerve of the man, she took a moment for his question to sink in. 'You appeared to be expecting someone called George?' he said. 'When you opened the door?' His brows lifted a millimetre in gentle query. 'You definitely weren't expecting me,' he pointed out, quite unnecessarily.

'Oh.' The man had a way of changing direction without warning. She'd line up her mind to cope with whatever he was saying, and then he'd throw her off by asking the most unexpected question. 'No.' She gathered herself. 'I thought you were my neighbour from across the hall. He's a regular "Have you got a cup of sugar?" merchant. Never short of things like sun-dried tomatoes, first pressing olive oil, buffalo mozzarella, but the basics seem to elude him.'

'Genuinely?' he asked, glancing at the simple Shaker wall clock. 'Or is it just an excuse to drop by, catch you when you're...' his gaze returned to her casual appearance, lingered for a moment, stirring up all kinds of forbidden longings—he was the enemy '...relaxing?'

'He's gay,' she said. Then wished she hadn't. It was none of Jordan Farraday's business what she did out of hours, when the store was closed, and the prospect of a lover arriving at any moment might have provided her with a lever to get rid of him. Except she'd blown that over dinner with her three years, two months, six days... 'I could be naked,' she said, lending just the smallest touch of regret to her voice, 'and he'd still only want a pint of milk.' India, uncomfortably aware that she was not wearing a bra beneath the thin T-shirt, that her breasts were responding noticeably to all those male pheromones that made the air bristle around him, wished she hadn't brought up the subject of nakedness. 'And I'm not relaxing. I'm working,' she said, before he said something she'd have to hate him for. More, that was, than she did already. His gaze finally drifted towards the files. 'So, come on,' she demanded, in her best no-nonsense manner, 'tell me what you've got in that box. You know you're dying to.'

By way of answer he crossed to the sofa, sat down and lifted the flaps on the box. Then he looked up, inviting her to come and see for herself. She remained where she was, at a safe distance. 'Well?' she demanded.

'Gareth—the security man at the store—found these wandering about the car park and didn't seem to know what to do them. He hoped to catch you when you came back for your car—apparently you usually look into the security office to say goodnight? But tonight for some reason you were in a hurry to get away...' He lifted one of those damn brows again, as if puzzled by her hasty exit. As if it had nothing to do with him.

Then he reached into the box and took out a handful

of white, black and ginger fur, and India forgot all about keeping her distance. 'Bonny's kittens?' She checked the box. 'Where's Bonny?' Then, with a sinking heart, she understood. If their mother had been around they wouldn't have been wandering about the car park.

'She hasn't been seen since yesterday. I'm sorry.'

'Gareth hasn't found her...?' She couldn't quite bring herself to say 'body'. But Jordan shook his head and she let out a tiny breath of relief. 'She disappears for days at a time. She once climbed into the back of a delivery truck and ended up in Lincolnshire.' One of the kittens opened its tiny mouth and mewed. 'Oh, bless.' She sat down beside him, taking one of the kittens and cradling it in the palm of her hand. 'They're so precious...'

'They're very small,' he said. 'Old enough to learn to lap, though, if someone had the time and patience to help them.'

'That's why you brought them to me?' She turned to look up at him and realised just how close he was. That he had a tiny scar on his cheekbone. That his dark eyes had tiny gold flecks in them. That, close up, the smile was deadly.

Her mouth dried.

'I can take them away again,' he said. 'If it's an inconvenience.'

'No!' She reached out, as if to reassure him. 'No, I'm glad you did.' The smooth cloth of his jacket was warm, the arm beneath it solid, strong, and she glanced up and saw that he was watching her, not the kittens he was holding. 'Well, thank you for bringing them. It was kind of you to bother.'

'I'm not kind, India. Never make that mistake.' And

this time there was no wry, self-mocking smile to soften the words. Only fathomless dark eyes that made her catch at her breath again, made her feel at once unbelievably young…and as old as time. She didn't want kindness. She wanted passion, power. She wanted to reach out and touch his mouth with her fingertips, wanted to lean into him, take him down into the soft cushions, see those gold flecks in his eyes blaze and then melt… 'As for thanking me…well, you might feel differently about that by morning.' She struggled to disentangle her thoughts from Jordan's words. 'They're babies,' he prompted gently. He was, it seemed, fully aware of her confusion. 'A full-time job.'

'Yes.' Her mind was free-wheeling, trying to catch a gear, and it took a long, confused moment before the cogs finally engaged. She carefully removed her hand from his arm, put the kitten back in the box, forced her desperate-to-be-kissed lips into a neat, don't-let-me-keep-you smile, and said, 'But don't worry. I'll manage.' She got up and headed for the kitchen.

Jordan remained where he was for a full minute. Scrubbed his face with his hands, dragged his fingers through his hair and counted backwards from a hundred while thinking of something seriously boring.

For a moment there he'd nearly blown it. India's eyes might be black as sin, velvet-black, with a soft melting look that betrayed every thought in her head, but this was not the moment to pick up the invitation he saw there. That the sex would be hot and exciting he had no doubt, but tomorrow she'd be angry with him, even angrier with herself, and she'd put up a firewall ten feet high. Sexual surrender was not enough. He wanted everything.

He'd take her to meltdown in his own good time, but first he wanted her emotional surrender. Wanted her on her knees, begging him to take everything, anything…

And if, right now, he was in desperate need of a cold shower—well, wasn't it well known that revenge was a dish best eaten cold?

Thanks to the kittens he'd managed to recover the ground he'd lost by that careless reference to her father…and then some. He loosened his tie, undid the top button of his shirt, picked up the box. Now it was time to earn some real Brownie points.

Not that spending an hour with India Claibourne was exactly a chore. She was still inclined to distrust him—he'd already discovered that she was clever—but he wasn't letting slip an opportunity to get beneath the barriers she'd erected. Not just against him, but, by her own confession, against any deep personal relationship with a man.

'I should have seen you to the door,' she said from the depths of a cupboard as he put the box on the kitchen island.

'Is that any way to treat a man who's offering to help?' He took off his jacket, hung it over the door, slipped his cufflinks and rolled up his sleeves.

'You're not helping me, Jordan. You just want to remind me that you're not going away.' As she stood up, turned to face him with a small jug in her hands, her eyes seemed huge, and for a moment Jordan felt transparent, as if she could read his mind, see right through into his cynical soul.

'Okay,' he said, fighting the temptation to cross the room, take the jug from her hands and turn the clock back five minutes—go back to where they'd been when she was on the point of surrender. 'Now we've established that I'm staying, shall we get on?' There would be plenty of time to get close at the weekend. Right now he didn't want her to feel crowded, threatened by his presence. 'How about if I see to the milk? Then I'll make some coffee while you're playing mother.'

'None of that sexist nonsense here, Mr Farraday. This store runs an equal opportunities policy.' She placed the jug into his hands. 'Daddy will have to do his share.'

'Can I employ a nanny?' The grin faded. Wrong answer. She'd been abandoned by her mother. Nannies must have figured large in her life. He caught a glimpse of the familiar, empty yawning gaps that were sometimes the heritage of a one-parent child... 'Unless you can find a broody feline we're going to have our hands full tomorrow.'

'We?'

'I'm here, aren't I?'

Yes, he was indisputably here. Taking over her kitchen the way he would take over Claibourne & Farraday unless she found a way to stop him. Taking over her with his lethal smile. Even now she was standing far too close, her hand still fixed to the jug, even though he was holding it safely.

India knew she should have walked him to the door, locked it behind him and put up the safety chain, but it had been a matter of urgency to put some distance between them. Do a little deep breathing. Cool off.

She should have gone straight for the cold shower and

stayed there, because in his shirtsleeves, tie loose about his neck, his dark hair uncharacteristically ruffled, he offered straight-to-hell temptation.

'Can we fit the management of a major department store around the needs of a family of motherless kittens?' he asked.

From the box, the kittens mewed, distracting her from thoughts so out of character that she thought she must be bewitched. She let go the jug, put some space between them.

'We?' she repeated, and hoped she conveyed an impression that he was a long way from getting his feet beneath her desk. 'I don't know about you, Jordan, but I certainly can,' she said, taking a carton of milk from the fridge. 'You know, this is why men are hopeless domestically,' she continued. 'They can't do anything without a plan. They're still conducting a time and motion study while a woman has finished and put her feet up.'

'It's because women refuse to organise themselves properly that they're so hopeless in business.'

'It's our flexibility' she contradicted, 'that makes us so good. We're so much better equipped to cope with life's sudden crises. Unlike men,' she added, 'who can't do anything without creating a three-act drama out of it.' Fine sentiments, but unfortunately the milk carton was determined to undermine her Miss Efficiency act by stubbornly refusing to open.

'I think perhaps you're confusing me with some other man,' he suggested. 'James Cawston, perhaps?' He took the carton from her, opened it without fuss—a wordless demonstration of his domestic skills—and poured some into the jug before putting it into the microwave to take the chill off. 'If he's like that, I can understand why you chose not to marry him.' He tested the milk, put it on for a few more seconds.

'You weren't listening, Jordan,' she said, leaving him to it and sliding onto a stool at the centre island. 'I didn't marry him because I'm already wed to the store.'

Jordan was listening and hearing rather more than she intended, he thought. 'Right,' he said, as if he wasn't convinced—well, he wasn't—and let it go.

'I thought you understood,' she said as he handed her the milk, settled on a stool beside her, his elbows propped on the work surface, his fingers laced together, his chin propped on his hands as he looked sideways at her. 'Are you telling me that you're not like that?'

'Like what? Am I a man who can't work without a plan? Or am I wed to my work?'

'Either.' She was apparently concentrating on the milk, testing the temperature with a knuckle, and there was only the deep burgundy perfection of her nail polish to link her to the career woman with whom he'd spent the day. But he wasn't fooled for a minute. And right on cue she glanced up, looked right at him. It was a look with a high-voltage punch. 'Both,' she said.

Her hair might be caught up in a cute mop on top of her head, her clothes well-worn favourites fit only for relaxing in the privacy of her own home, but he'd seen the dates on the files she was looking at. They were thirty years old. And the top one at least—according to the title—contained correspondence with C&F's lawyers.

She hadn't given up trying to obstruct him. She wouldn't give up her fight to hang onto the store while there was a breath left in body. Three months ago, a week ago, yesterday, even, to have had this confirmation of how much she cared would have pleased him. Right at this moment he could only see the waste…

'The first casualty in any battle is the plan, India.' His plan had been to launch a charm offensive. Disarm the lady. Have her open the door to Claibourne & Farraday and invite him in, his charm increasing in direct proportion to his ruthlessness. He'd learned a lot watching Peter Claibourne in action.

But there was always the unexpected to be taken into consideration. He knew she was desirable, unattached, available and—with both her sisters, her allies, falling for the enemy and jumping ship—very much alone.

What he hadn't expected was that he would like her. But then Peter Claibourne had probably liked his mother. Certainly enough to spend the night with her.

And anything Peter Claibourne could do, he could top… 'As for my work—well, I wouldn't describe it as a marriage, but I give it my full attention.'

'Your full and undivided attention?'

'If you're suggesting I don't have time for the additional burden of Claibourne & Farraday, I'm afraid I'm going to have to disappoint you. I always have time for those things that are important to me.'

'In other words you're a workaholic?'

'Not exactly.' His work didn't exclude other interests, but maybe it was a barrier against deep involvement. Against hurt. 'But a man has to work.'

'If you never worked again you could live in luxury on the profits made by Claibourne & Farraday.'

'You don't have to work either,' he pointed out. Which was just as well, since she'd soon be out of a job. He might like her, might do rather more than that, but that didn't change anything. 'And I'm offering the same deal. Sit back, take the profits and enjoy yourself.'

She dipped her thumb into the milk and offered it to one of the kittens. 'It would seem that we're more alike than you're prepared to admit,' she suggested, glancing up, challenging him. Then after a moment she gave her attention to the eagerly nuzzling kitten.

He picked up a tiny ball of fluff, dipped his thumb in the milk and followed her example.

'Have you ever been married, Jordan?' He glanced up. 'Lived with anyone?'

'I assumed you'd done a little background research on us.'

'I did, but I was interested in your working life, not gossip.' When he raised an eyebrow, she said, 'This is just making conversation.'

He shrugged. 'I've never actually made it up the aisle. I came close once, about ten years ago, but Ellie couldn't understand why I found work more interesting than lazing on a beach somewhere, or partying at a fashionable ski resort.'

'She thought your job should be the hobby?' she asked, lifting her expressive brows in sympathy.

Well, she'd been there more recently—three years, two months and six days ago, to be precise. Maybe she was right about them being alike.

'When I explained that it was never going to be that way she found someone else with more time to devote to pleasure.'

'Your own James Cawston...' she said, putting down the first kitten and picking up its sibling.

'I wouldn't have described her in that way exactly,' he said drily, as he recalled the beautiful girl he'd so nearly married. 'But, like him, she did have the good sense to recognise it wasn't going to work and walk away.'

'It doesn't make it any easier, does it?' Something in her voice made him look up. She was looking at him intently, and he realised that he'd hit on a tender spot. He knew what it was.

'No,' he said. 'It's still rejection, no matter how well meant. The head can see the sense of it, but...' He couldn't quite bring himself to make any reference to his heart. He'd got used to thinking of himself without one. 'The fact that she later married someone else who was pretty much a mirror image of me suggests that maybe it wasn't entirely the work that was the problem.'

'There isn't a man alive who could be described as a mirror image of you, Jordan.'

He offered the wryest of smiles. 'Perhaps we're both lost causes.'

'Maybe your secretary's crazy idea has more merit than we thought.' He frowned. 'We should marry each other since no one else will have us.' Was that the tiniest shake in her voice? 'We could be work-obsessive together.'

Now he'd met India Claibourne the idea didn't seem anywhere nearly as crazy, he discovered. 'Is that a proposal?'

'Only if you're going to say yes,' she said, then laughed, just to make sure he knew she was joking.

'What will you do?'

'Do?' Her long, slender neck curved invitingly as she bent over the kitten held to her breast, the soft, worn T-shirt sliding over her shoulder to expose flawless silken skin and confirm what he already knew. That beneath it she was naked.

This morning, when he'd first set eyes on her, she'd stunned him with her beauty, her poise. This evening she was bereft of artifice—with nothing more than the bloom of her skin, her body more revealed than concealed beneath the soft clothes she was wearing, the bright candour of her dark eyes—and he discovered that she was capable of doing much, much more.

She exposed his cynicism to the raw air and made it ache.

Well, he could live with that, but what was fresh, unexpected, was the way, by just looking up at him, fixing him with her level, disbelieving gaze, she was able to heat something buried deep inside him, quicken his desire.

He'd always been in total control of his emotions. Yesterday he'd confidently assured Christine of his single-mindedness. That gaining control of a department store was the only thing on his mind. Yet even while he'd been looking for ways to get beneath India Claibourne's skin she had somehow managed to slip beneath his.

She glanced up when he didn't answer, her lips softly curved in a natural smile, her dewy fresh skin an invitation to touch, to kiss.

'Do?' she prompted. The smile faded when he didn't reply, and she put the kitten back in the box, sliding from the stool to stand and face him. 'At the end of the month? What will I do when you've got Claibourne & Farraday and I'm standing on the pavement with the contents of my desk in a cardboard box? That's what you meant, isn't it?'

He wasn't sure why he was so bothered. It was none

of his concern what she did after he'd taken Claibourne & Farraday away from her. And yet there was no backing away from it. That was what he'd meant.

'You must have given it some consideration,' he said.

'Must I? Why?' Her voice was level, even, and for a moment he thought she was seriously inviting a response from him. But before he could offer one she answered her own question. 'Because you're JD Farraday and you're going to win. That's what you do, isn't it? Always.' And this time her smile was about as genuine as fool's gold. 'You see? I may not have dredged the gossip columns for the last thirty years, but I've done my homework. The important stuff.' Then, 'Well? Is that it?'

'What exactly are you asking me?'

'Why you've got the nerve to think you should take control of Claibourne & Farraday just because you're a man.' She hadn't raised her voice, but lowered it, forcing him to listen closely to what she had to say. 'And heaven help me for daring to think that I can challenge you at your own game.'

'India—'

'Forget that I'm better qualified, that I've lived and breathed Claibourne & Farraday since I was old enough to say the words. Forget that I know what I'm doing and you don't know the first thing about running a department store. That this is the twenty-first century and deciding who's going to run a business on the grounds of sex and age is so unbelievable that it will be laughed out of court—'

'If it goes to court we've both lost,' he said sharply, breaking into this stream of comments—every one of which, under other circumstances, he would have been applauding. 'We might as well sell out now.'

His remark was greeted with a moment of total silence. Then she said, 'Had an offer, have you?'

He'd done it again. He'd got her relaxed, smiling, forgetting the dispute between them, and then, when he'd thought he was getting close, a careless phrase had destroyed the mood. Except he was never that careless. He was being ambushed by his subconscious. The small still voice of conscience that was telling him to stop, walk away.

'One too good to turn down?' she pressed.

'Haven't you?' he asked, but he already knew the answer. The Claibournes had received plenty of offers over the years, but they hadn't been interested. That was why, the minute Peter Claibourne had been rushed into Intensive Care, the giant retail groups had turned to him. A man without an ounce of sentiment in his body.

He put the kitten back in the box, eased himself from the stool. The kittens had provided a way into her home, an opportunity to slip beneath her guard, but he'd thrown away the advantage, brought bright pink patches of anger to her cheeks. He'd won this round—just like the previous one in the restaurant. Breaking down her reserve. Making her see him as something more than an enemy. And both times he'd thrown it carelessly away. But this time she couldn't get into her car and drive away from him.

He captured a strand of hair that had fallen over her eyes and tucked it safely behind her ear, before sliding his fingers beneath her chin, forcing her to look up at him.

'You should always have an exit plan, India,' he said. Good advice under any circumstances. Advice he'd do well to heed. But the exit could go hang for a moment. Right now he was going to do something he'd been anticipating ever since she'd proposed this shadowing scheme.

What his body had been urging him to do since he'd first set eyes on her that morning.

He kissed her.

CHAPTER SIX

INDIA read his intent in the sudden stillness of his body, the darkening of his eyes, but even while her brain was sending urgent *Move!* signals to her legs it was already too late.

Jordan's hand shifted from her chin, opened to capture her head, cupping it in his palm while his sexy mouth descended with tormenting slowness before it brushed softly against her own.

Sizzling, searingly sweet, her lips parted hungrily beneath the sensory overload, and at that point her legs weren't listening to anyone. Even as her brain surrendered and intuition kicked in they were buckling weakly, so that she leaned instinctively into his body for support.

His impulse to kiss her was at once so perfect, so true, that for a moment he closed his eyes to shut out the look of sweet surprise that widened hers, caught his breath at the physical kickback from the soft, clinging warmth of her mouth as India responded instinctively to his touch.

How long was it since a woman had left him feeling so weak? His first kiss... First time...

And in that instant he knew that any pretence of being the one single-mindedly in control had just flown out of the window. He'd kissed her not as part of some cynical manoeuvre to seduce her, steal her heart and her soul, along with her department store, but because that was what he'd wanted to do...more than anything else in the world.

Kissing India Claibourne had certainly opened his eyes, opened them wide. Looking into hers—startled, a little confused as her lips clung to his—he'd believed, for a heartbeat, that the heady rush making him feel ten feet tall was victory. The chilling backwash of reality was just as swift.

Impulse. He had kissed her on an impulse, he realised. What had happened to his awareness? Where was his much-vaunted control? Twenty minutes ago he'd been putting distance between the two of them, knowing that it would be a mistake to move too quickly, that she'd suspect his motives and put up her defences. And then, impulsively, he'd blown it.

That was what you got for using sex as a weapon. It could turn on you without warning, leaving you the one with an unfulfilled ache, a hollow feeling of regret, as you took a precious moment and turned it to your own advantage.

Still close enough to see the tiny glints of amber glowing softly in her eyes, he moved swiftly, giving her no time to think, reclaim the high ground and reject him. 'Give it some thought,' he said, releasing her, leaving her to decide whether it was the exit strategy or his kiss that should occupy her mind.

About to say something, she changed her mind and instead took a step back.

He should already have said good night and be on the way to the door, yet still he lingered. 'How will you manage? Tomorrow.'

'Tomorrow?' She seemed confused, disorientated, and

it was impossible to miss the fact that her breath was coming rather faster, her breasts gratifyingly peaked against the give-away softness of her T-shirt. Could it be that she'd been as entranced with his kiss as he'd been with her response? The words, the tone of her voice had been giving him a red signal, but everything else appeared to be on amber and heading for green.

He shut the thought down before it overwhelmed him, concentrating instead on the advantage gained. The satisfaction of discovering that he hadn't lost quite as much ground as he thought.

'The kittens,' he said. 'They'll need constant attention.'

'I...um...guess I'll just have to use my managerial skills and organise something,' she said, turning as if to look at them, but gripping the back of the stool, her knuckles white.

'I wish...' He hesitated, but as she glanced at him he shook his head, leaving her to wonder what exactly it was that he wished. Maybe when she'd worked it out she could tell him. 'I'll see you tomorrow, India.'

'Please...' it was his turn to wait '...shut the door on your way out.'

Polite, distant, and this time her invitation to leave was as blunt as a hand on the collar and a boot to the backside.

India jumped as the front door shut with a sharp click. He'd taken her by surprise. That could be the only possible explanation why she'd stood there and let him get away with that kiss.

She swallowed, took a deep, steadying breath.

And anyway, to describe it as a *kiss*, she told herself, was undoubtedly an exaggeration. It had been scarcely more than a touch of his lips to hers. It was certainly nothing to be getting hot under the collar about. So why was she? Hot.

She rubbed the back of her hand across her forehead, down over her neck. Steaming hot. And bothered as hell. Her lips tingling and swollen as if she'd been necking all evening like some teenager in the back row of the cinema.

How had he done that? With just the touch of his mouth to hers?

What did these Farraday men have that ordinary mortals seemed to lack? First Romana, then Flora had fallen for the Farraday charm, and now she was letting Jordan walk into her apartment and take liberties that very few men would even have dared attempt, let alone get away with.

Did they simply have to reach out and touch for women to fall in lust with them? Fall into love with them, she corrected herself. Romana and Flora were women for whom nothing less would do. It would have to be true love—the world-well-lost sort of love—to capture their hearts.

Except that for her it would not be the world well lost but Claibourne & Farraday. And for a moment there she'd been prepared to lay down her arms and surrender. Just like her sisters.

Which was ridiculous. She hadn't fallen in anything with Jordan Farraday. He was a sizzlingly attractive man, no doubt; her lips were still hot from his touch. But this wasn't about love, or even lust. It was the heightened awareness of a winner-takes-all situation momentarily boiling over into something more. She'd been edgily aware of him at her shoulder all day. Even when he was out of her line of sight his presence was so disturbingly *physical* that she could feel it.

Maintaining concentration had been difficult. She'd wanted to keep looking around to check that her imagination wasn't playing tricks on her. That if she could just catch him unawares she'd see that he was just another man.

She lifted her fingers to her mouth and was prepared to admit, in the privacy of her own kitchen, that Jordan Farraday wasn't 'just' anything.

The kittens were mewing for attention and she picked one up, holding it at eye level. She'd been too concerned about them to wonder why he'd taken the trouble to bring them to her. But suddenly it was as clear as crystal.

'You're not really a kitten,' she told the scrap of fur. 'You're a Trojan horse. Welcomed with open arms, made a fuss of, and all the time you're just a ruse to bring the enemy inside the gates.' She had to admire a man who could take such swift advantage of an unexpected opportunity.

He was different, all right. He deserved an award as cynic of the week.

What she deserved for being taken in—even temporarily—by such a ploy was something else.

Jordan sat at the wheel of his car, disconcerted to find that he was shaking. One day at her side, seduced by the silken sway of her hair, a scent he couldn't quite pin down, had left him ragged with unfulfilled desire. Christine was right. If he didn't take care, a week of this would have him on his knees. And happy to be there.

* * *

India made some telephone calls, then, having settled her orphans, she took the files to bed and made herself comfortable; it was going to be a long night. Her eyes grew heavy as she trawled through the endless correspondence, the dense legal jargon, too tired to make sense of the discovery that Kitty Farraday had fought to hold on to the store after her father's death…

A particularly heavy file woke her with a start as it slid to the floor. For a moment she lay back against the pillows, trying to convince herself that she could leave it until tomorrow, but even as she turned over and closed her eyes she knew she'd never get back to sleep.

And as she climbed out of bed she told herself that bags under her eyes weren't all bad news. They were so puffy and unattractive that they'd keep Jordan Farraday's mind firmly on the business side of their partnership.

As she began to gather up the scattered papers she discovered the thought wasn't as consoling as it should have been. It might have bothered her more if at that moment she hadn't picked up a folded, yellowing sheet of paper. It was a handwritten note, not addressed to anyone, or signed.

The reason for that became obvious as she read it. It was clearly legal advice, but not the kind that any lawyer would be willing to put his name to.

Since I have not seen the letter, I cannot offer an opinion on its probity, only warn that its appearance would cause grave difficulties if disclosed at this time. Circumstances might arise at some point in the future, however, that would make breaking the 'golden share' covenant imperative. I would advise safe keeping.

Letter? India frowned. What letter? She went through the file from front to back, this time wide awake. There was nothing. She hadn't really expected there would be.

But somewhere there was a letter that would break the golden share agreement. All she had to do was find it.

Jordan pulled into his assigned parking space just before eight o'clock. He'd finally given up trying to sleep, and at five he'd been in his own office. There was nothing like work to take the mind off physical yearnings. The kind that had no prospect of being fulfilled.

It required a clear head to plot the seduction and downfall of a woman. Clouded by desire, it could all so easily go wrong. Before he knew it, a man could find himself falling in love.

There was no sign of India's car. Presumably, after a night of playing mother to the kittens, she'd overslept. Under any other circumstances he'd have taken great pleasure in giving her a wake-up call. Reminding her of her inadequacies.

But she was going to be mad enough with herself for being late, for leaving him to walk through the alterations with the surveyor, he decided as he made his way up to the top floor. It was quite unnecessary for him to heap coals on the bonfire.

Or maybe it was the thought of her answering the telephone, her eyes slumberous, her dark hair tousled and spread over the pillow. He knew he'd rather be lying beside her as she surfaced slowly to full consciousness, witnessing the soft curve of her smile as she saw him there, than on the other end of a phone line making her frown.

'Good morning, JD,' Sally said as he walked into her office.

He covered his surprise at seeing her at her desk. 'Good morning, Sally. Do you normally start this early?' he asked.

'It depends,' she replied enigmatically, and yawned. 'Would you like coffee?'

'Thanks, but I'll leave it until after the surveyor's given us the tour.'

'Ah.' The flat tone of her voice was enough to warn him that appearances could be deceptive, that he should take nothing for granted. 'You've missed the surveyor, I'm afraid. The meeting was brought forward to seven.'

He smothered the hot flare of irritation. While he'd been giving his imagination free rein India Claibourne had been one step ahead of him. 'At whose request?'

'I couldn't say.' Wouldn't, more like. 'Indie asked me to apologise on her behalf for getting you out of bed so early on a fool's errand. She would have phoned, but she didn't have your number at home and apparently it isn't listed.'

'And where is she now? Gone back to her own bed to catch up on her lost sleep?'

'Excuse me?'

He recognised a stonewalling secretary when he met one. 'What time will she be coming back?'

'Oh, right. Well, after the surveyor left she went downstairs to go over the plans for refurbishing the book department with the maintenance manager.'

'Are you sure? Her car isn't in the car park.'

'She left it at the garage on her way in. For a service.' She glanced at her watch. 'You'll probably find her in the staff canteen now, getting some breakfast. Since she had such an early start. Do you want me to bleep her and let her know you've arrived?'

'That won't be necessary. I'll join her there. If you'll point the way?'

'It's down in the basement.' And she gave him directions. He walked down through the store. Not open for another couple of hours it was, nevertheless, a hive of activity. Cleaners were busy putting on the gloss, staff in Glassware were unpacking a consignment of Lalique angel-fish and assembling a glittering new display. Everything had to be perfect when the doors opened to the public, but the perfection had to be attained without visible effort.

His mother had told him how a cardboard box left on the sales floor after the store had opened would bring down the wrath of a department head: being a Farraday hadn't shielded her from that.

It was the first time he'd seen it for himself. Unlike his mother—or the Claibourne girls—he'd never worked in the store in school and university vacations. It was like a theatre in the frantic moments before the curtain went up, he thought. And for the first time he caught a spark of the excitement, the mystery. The magic.

He found the canteen, bought himself a cup of coffee and crossed to a table in the corner where India was nibbling at a slice of toast while she read through a file, apparently oblivious to his presence.

She looked up when he put down the cup he was carrying, hooking a dark, silky wing of hair behind her ear, exposing the satin skin of her neck that had been such a feature of his disturbed night. 'Good morning, Jordan.'

He said nothing, but instead extracted a business card from his wallet and placed it on top of the file she was reading. 'My telephone number,' he said, holding it there with the tip of one finger while he spoke. 'For future reference.'

Not that there was going to be a future.

She ignored it. 'Sally phoned to say you were on your way down ten minutes ago. Did you get lost?'

'No, I walked down through the store. I've never been here when it's closed.' He tapped the file in front of her, before sitting in the chair opposite. 'And, since I anticipated Sally's call, I thought I'd give you time to put away anything you didn't want me to see.' Not that she'd find anything to help her. No matter how old and dusty the file.

'What a gentleman,' she said, and rewarded him with the briefest smile. 'I'm afraid this is nothing more exciting than the sales figures for swimwear.' She made an open gesture over the file. 'Would you like to see how well we're doing?'

'I can wait until the end of the month.'

'Well, just say if you change your mind,' she said, then indicated her plate. 'Do help yourself to toast. It's freshly made. Or maybe you'd prefer something more substantial? Breakfast is the most important meal of the day.'

'I had mine a couple of hours ago,' he said, taking a slice. 'Before I went into my office. If you'd let me know this was going to be a wasted journey I could still be there, doing something useful.'

'But you'd have missed the pleasure of walking through the store before the doors open. I always think it's rather like a great orchestra tuning up…' She stopped, made a dismissive little gesture with her fingers. 'A little fanciful for a hard-headed business tycoon, no doubt.'

'No doubt,' he replied.

She regarded him thoughtfully, clearly aware that his response was open to more than one interpretation. He loved that quickness. If she had any kind of case, she'd be a formidable opponent.

'I'm sorry you feel you've wasted your time, Jordan. If I'd known you would be in your office I'd have called you.' Then, after an almost imperceptible pause, 'Although I was under the impression that you wanted to shadow me throughout my working day. You've already missed an hour.' Oh, right. She was sorry. And she was happy to have him at her side twelve hours a day. And he was the Maharajah of Bengal. 'Do you normally start so early?' she asked.

'I like the office when it's quiet. Unlike you, however, I don't expect my secretary to join me at dawn.'

'Hardly dawn,' she protested. 'The sun was well above the horizon when I left home. Besides, Sally came in early on a flexi-working arrangement. She's taking the afternoon off.' His doubt must have shown because she said, 'Personnel will confirm that it was arranged weeks ago if you don't believe me.' Then added, 'Although why I should lie…'

'And the surveyor?' he said, ignoring her slightly puzzled frown. It was beautifully done, but he knew when he was being given the runaround. 'What's the story there?'

'Oh, poor man. He rang me at six. He broke a tooth last night and his dentist offered to fit him in with an emergency appointment before his surgery.'

And she looked at him with those clear bright eyes that were hovering on the brink of a smile, defying him to challenge her.

'Flexi-time all round, then.'

'I'm very much in favour of flexibility,' she replied, and she picked up the last piece of toast and bit into it with even white teeth.

For a woman who'd been up half the night with three immature kittens she looked fresh, wide awake and good enough to eat in a simply cut black jersey top, long sleeves pushed up a little to expose slender wrists. Arouna one of them was a plain, workmanlike gold wristwatch. Apart from that, and small gold earrings, she wore no jewellery. But a softly coiled silk chiffon scarf lay around her throat. Burgundy and gold. He had the feeling that he'd be seeing a lot of that particular colour scheme during the next four weeks.

And it would not be one day less, he promised himself. There was no way he was going to allow Miss India Claibourne to get away with giving him the run-around. He was going to stamp his authority on this store—and upon her—before he showed her the door.

Even as he thought it, he could almost hear his secretary's voice mocking him. Warning him not to eat or drink anything. Because the Claibourne girls were witches.

Some witch. Despite her sophistication, the perfect grooming, he saw only the girl with her hair escaping from a topknot, a grey washed-thin T-shirt sliding from her shoulder, her breasts peaked eagerly against them, soft bare lips lifted to him…

The memory sparked a flood of heat that left him gasping.

'Did you say something?' she asked. He shook his head, tried to think of something boring. There wasn't anything boring enough… 'I'm sorry I couldn't get in touch to let you know.' She picked up his card, ran her thumb over the lettering. It felt as if she was stroking his skin. 'About the surveyor,' she added, in case he wasn't quite clear what exactly she was apologising for. 'It must be quite a problem, fitting us in around your own business commitments.'

'Don't give it another thought,' he said.

'I think one of us should. Don't you?' With that she glanced at her wristwatch, then, after stowing his card away carefully in her handbag and closing the file in front of her, stood up. 'Right. Time to get on.' She glanced at his cup. 'Do you want to stay and finish that?'

'No, I was just being sociable.'

He brushed the toast crumbs from his fingers.

'Then let's go.' And she gave him a smile so bright that it set his teeth on edge. She was up to something.

'Who's looking after the kittens?' he asked.

Her smile, impossibly, increased by several megawatts. 'Do you want the long story or the short one?' she asked as she headed towards the door.

'Let's start with the short one.'

'They're back with their mother.'

'What?'

'You should have started with the long one,' she advised him. 'It's always quickest in the long run.' He held the door for her, then crossed to the lift, pressing the button to summon it. She walked right on by. 'We're going to the ground floor,' she explained. 'Only one flight.'

'The kittens?' he repeated, falling in beside her.

'Oh, yes. Did I tell you that Bonny once took a truck ride all the way to Lincolnshire?'

She knew, he decided. She'd worked out why he'd taken the kittens to her apartment and she was taking enormous pleasure in spinning out the story, explaining why his plan to present himself as a truly warm and caring human being hadn't worked.

'You did. Took a liking to the place, did she? Went back for another look?'

'Thankfully—for the kittens' sake—this time she didn't get so far. After you left I phoned the security desk and had the officer on duty check all the day's deliveries—they're logged in and out,' she explained. 'And then call all the depots and ask them to check their vans. She wasn't far. At the fishmarket, in fact. Kittens and mother reunited in hours.'

'That's good news.' Then, pausing at the foot of the stairs, 'You don't look as if you've been up half the night.'

'Well, thank you, Jordan, but I can take no credit for that. I was in bed with a good file before twelve. All I had to do was make one call to Security, then I delivered the kittens to George. I've lost count of the times he's promised that one day he'll do something to thank me for always being there with a loaf of bread or a cup of sugar when he needs one.'

'Every time he needed a loaf of bread, I imagine.'

'You're right,' she said. And laughed, as if he'd said

something really funny. 'Well, last night was his chance to be a hero.'

'Well, good for George.'

'It wasn't really that much of an imposition. He's a chronic insomniac. And he loves cats.' She looked up at him, wide eyes innocent as those tiny kittens'. 'I don't suppose you'd like one of Bonny's kittens, would you? It's always a problem finding them good homes,' she said. 'We try to keep them in the, um, "family".' For a moment he thought she was going to spoil the performance by laughing again. But she covered the slip with a little cough and set off up the stairs.

He was about to suggest neutering as the sensible solution when an alternative offered itself to his fertile mind. She'd been having fun at his expense for quite long enough. It was time to turn the tables.

'I'll make a deal with you.' She didn't respond, simply waited, expecting him to wriggle and prepared to enjoy the spectacle, no doubt. 'If I offer all of Bonny's kittens the kind of home that most cats can only dream about—'

'All three of them?' She gave him a dubious look from beneath her long dark lashes.

'Kittens need company. They'll be able to stay together. They'll have a proper garden, fenceposts to scratch without anyone yelling at them. Small mammals to slaughter in abundance. Cat heaven.'

'It certainly sounds that way,' she agreed. Then, 'If?'

'If?'

'You said it was a deal. *If* you give the kittens a home, you said. The word implies you expect something in return.'

'Oh, yes. But it's nothing onerous or difficult, I promise

you.' And it was his turn to switch on the megawatt smile. 'I just want you to upgrade your "definitely maybe" response to my invitation to join me for the weekend—make it a firm commitment. Two days out of your life in return for a lifetime of bliss for Bonny's kittens. What do you say?'

She'd been doing so well, India thought. Congratulating herself on seeing—if somewhat belatedly—through his cynical use of three little kittens to slip beneath her guard.

He'd left the kiss a fraction undercooked to completely distract her, however. Or maybe he was confident that, like her sisters, she would crumple beneath the killer effect of the Farraday sex appeal and abandon the retail sector in favour of his bed.

She stopped that train of thought in its tracks. He'd been the one who'd stopped the kiss, not her. If he'd waited for her to object they'd have still been there...

Get a grip! She'd handled the kittens; she could handle him. He wasn't infallible. She'd eventually caught on to what he was up to last night. He'd used them. Now it was her turn.

But Jordan Farraday was not a man to be easily embarrassed. On the contrary, he'd taken her outrageous lie about the difficulty of finding homes for the kittens—there was in actual fact a waiting list for them—and he'd turned it right around, stamped 'return to sender'.

'What do you say?' He stopped on the half-landing, blocking her way, insisting upon an answer.

'I say...' she began, then kept him waiting while she took a slow, deep breath, 'I say, show me this paradise for moggies and then I'll think about it.'

His smile was the full works. Little pouches beneath the eyes—the test of a genuine smile. Teeth...seriously good teeth. A shark would envy teeth like that. Those sexy creases that deepened in his cheeks. A knockout, one hundred per cent smile, in fact. And the effect was...knockout. She was going to have to start carrying around one of those little canisters of oxygen...

'Then we have a deal.'

'We do?' Maybe it was the effect of his smile, but she had no recollection of reaching the bottom line.

'You can inspect "paradise" this weekend,' he told her, and finally, far too late to back-pedal, she caught on.

'You mean you're off-loading the kittens on your unsuspecting friend? The one with his own personal cricket pitch and a heated swimming pool?'

'I said I'd offer them a home, India. I don't recall specifying whose home it would be. There'll be no objection; you have my personal guarantee.' And he offered her his hand. 'We have a deal?' he pressed.

She didn't say a word. She'd already talked herself into enough trouble. But she thought something very rude as she reached out, intending the briefest of handshakes.

His fingers closed about her hand in a cool, firm grip. The kind that evinced dependability, probity, candour. And she was forced to remind herself that a good, confidence-inspiring handshake was an essential for a man who spent his life handling vast sums of money.

It made no difference. She knew it was the measure of the man. And for the first time she found herself truly regretting their dispute. Wishing they were on the same side. He could bring so much to the store in experience, enterprise, originality.

If she could find the mysterious letter, he still might.

'I walked into that one, didn't I?' she said, her smile not entirely forced, as she accepted defeat gracefully.

'I hoped you would. You won't regret it,' he promised. 'I'll make it my personal mission to ensure you enjoy yourself.'

'I'll hold you to that,' she assured him, cooling the smile. It wouldn't do to appear too eager. He had no way of knowing that there was, somewhere, waiting to be unearthed at this 'imperative' moment, a letter that would break the agreement. A letter that would give her a fair chance of winning. On truly equal terms. All she had to do was find it.

All! She had no idea who'd written the note. Or to whom. No idea what this unknown someone might have considered 'safe keeping'. But for now it would be safer if he thought he was the one with the upper hand and she was clutching at straws.

It would have helped if her father hadn't chosen this moment to disappear from the face of the earth, with his mobile phone switched off, his e-mails left unanswered.

Sally's advice to 'do a Claibourne' on Jordan surfaced briefly. As a desperate holding action. She firmly quashed the idea as preposterous. She hadn't got the least idea how to make any man fall in love with her. She wasn't a natural flirt, like Romana. She didn't have him isolated on a tropical island paradise, like Flora. And Jordan wasn't the kind of man to be easily taken in. It would have to be the real thing…

'Just ensure that I've got a room to myself,' she said—just in case he decided his 'personal mission' to ensure her enjoyment included making up for her wasted three years, two months and... No, she'd lost count of the days. 'Having to bunk with the cricket team would not be my idea of a good time. Now, I really must get on if I'm going away for the weekend.' But he didn't move. And he didn't let go of her hand.

'Is that the way the Claibournes close a deal?' he asked.

'I'm sorry? Did you want something in writing?'

'Nothing so formal.' He raised her hand to his lips, and she knew what was coming. But even while she was sending frantic signals to her brain he raised his free hand, sliding his fingers through her hair, cradling her head, holding her captive. 'I had in mind something more along the lines of that old song title...you remember the one?' He didn't wait for her to confirm or deny it, but instead gave her his very personal interpretation of sealing an agreement with a kiss.

This time there were no half measures. No playful brushing of lips in an opening gambit that offered the opportunity for a swift check—should the opponent wish to end the game.

This was a kiss intended to make a lasting impression, one that her lips responded to instinctively, ignoring the belated stop signals flashing from her brain. They'd been given a foretaste of something wonderful last night, a promise that there was more to come. They were too busy collecting on that promise to let anything as boring as common sense stop their fun. And Jordan Farraday took full advantage of their decision to go it alone.

His mouth was cool against hers. Cool and completely in control. His tongue was like silk as he took his own sweet time about extracting her promise. While she was hot, flushed and vibrantly aware that every cell in her body was being given a wake-up call. Only when she was captivated, boneless, breathless, did he finally lift his head and offer her his lazy half smile—the one that made her want to smile right back.

Lost for words she might have been, but worse, far worse, was the contented little tell-tale sigh that escaped her lips.

'*Now,*' he said, 'we have a deal.'

CHAPTER SEVEN

INDIA was speechless. Not that it mattered—if she could have thought of anything to say she wouldn't have had the breath to say it.

Taking advantage of the situation, Jordan took her by the arm as he steered her up the remaining stairs and through the door into the Cosmetic and perfume departments.

'So,' he said, 'what are we doing here?'

She'd forgotten. For the life of her she couldn't remember. Her mind, usually razor-sharp, had been reduced to a squishy mass of marshmallow. Fortunately the department head spotted her and came to her rescue. 'Good morning, Miss Claibourne. We're all set up, if you'd like to come and see.'

She introduced Jordan, although it was clear the man already knew who he was—and what he was doing in the store. 'We're introducing a new line of cosmetics. Something for the younger customers,' he explained, addressing himself to Jordan. 'It's a major market and rather a new one for us. Miss Claibourne has been making huge strides in getting the 15-25-year-old age group through the doors. Today we're offering decorative henna painting as an incentive.'

'Buy one, get one free?' Jordan suggested.

India, breath restored, had had quite enough of this

cosy all-men-together chat. 'Claibourne & Farraday is not a supermarket,' she said.

'The henna painting is simply a draw, Mr Farraday,' the department manager intervened swiftly.

The man clearly thought he was talking to the next Managing Director of Claibourne & Farraday, and was intent on making a good impression. Did everyone believe that? she wondered. Were all her staff busy mentally adjusting their allegiances even as she stood there? 'It's very popular,' she said, determined to regain command.

'Is it? Show me,' Jordan said. He still had her elbow gripped firmly in his hand and he crossed to the waiting chair and lowered her into it. Her legs, not quite recovered from the force of his kiss, buckled without resistance. He glanced at the henna artist. 'Miss Claibourne will make the perfect guinea pig. She has lovely hands.' As if to demonstrate, he took one of them, palm up, straightening her fingers with his thumb in a gesture that was pure caress and sent shock waves of desire to her already sensitised body. Did he know what he was *doing*?

He seemed to be looking at her palm for ever before he turned her hand over, and for one heart-stopping moment she thought he was going to repeat his courtly gesture and lift it to his lips. Right here. In front of her staff. A demonstration of his power...his control.

'Miss Claibourne has always been a great ambassador for the store.' The department head's smooth compliment short-circuited the static build-up in the air around them.

'I don't doubt it.' And, letting her go, Jordan stepped back to allow the artist to set to work.

Fleetingly, she was tempted. Tempted just to sit back and have exotic designs painted onto her hands like some pampered harem creature. Her hands painted, her body anointed with sweet scented oils, then wrapped in silk and delivered to the Sultan. A sultan with Jordan Farraday's face.

She gave a little gasp as common sense reasserted itself. 'It's an interesting idea, but I'll pass,' she said firmly. And, gripping the arms of the chair, she pushed herself to her feet. 'If you'll excuse me,' she said, and began to walk quickly in the direction of the nearest escalator.

'Where are you going?' She hadn't gone three yards before he was beside her. His voice demanded her attention. As if he was already in control. Well, he wasn't in control of her.

'I'm going to powder my nose, Jordan.' Or, roughly translated, she was grabbing a breathing space to take a healthy dousing in cold water. Walking—running—away from him while she was still in control of her senses. 'I'd invite you along, so that you can see how the other half do it, but the other occupants might not take kindly to your presence.'

'I thought there were washroom facilities on a lavish scale for the directors on the top floor. A private bathroom for every office.'

'Niall told you that, did he?'

'No,' he said. 'Niall took one look at your sister and forgot I existed.'

'What a pity she isn't here now, to work the same trick for me.' Make her forget that her lips were still throbbing from the kiss he'd taken without so much as by your leave. Treating them as if they were his personal help-yourself counter in a sweet shop. Make her forget that intimate caress as he'd stroked his thumb over her hand, sending shivers of anticipation to every part of her body. She'd been scared of what he might do to her beloved store. Suddenly the fear was on a deeper, more personal level. What might he do to *her*?

The answer, right now, appeared to be nothing. A muscle moved in the corner of his mouth. It might have been a suppressed smile; more likely bitten-back irritation that his kiss hadn't had a more lasting impact. That was all. There was no other visible or verbal reaction.

She realised she'd been holding her breath, waiting for an explosion that hadn't come. She wanted him to explode, lose control, as she'd so nearly done. Forget 'doing a Claibourne'. She'd be better advised to ensure that he didn't use the Farraday magic to sweep her off her feet.

'You're right, of course. There were private bathrooms installed in each of the director's offices—with no expense spared—by your grandfather,' she said, edgily sweeping her hair behind her ear.

'Don't do that,' he said, reaching up to free it, let it swing back over her cheek, over his fingers that lingered for moment. 'It's perfect just the way it is.' Then, 'I remember them.'

'What?'

'The bathrooms.'

'I didn't think you'd ever been here. Behind the scenes.'

'Not for a very long time,' he admitted. 'But my mother had one of those offices. I did those visits to Santa when I was a small boy, just like you. Came to be fitted for my first school clothes.'

She tried to imagine Jordan as a small boy. She couldn't do it. 'Your mother? What did she do?' But, recalling the letters in the old files, she knew the answer even before the question had escaped.

'Dreamed dreams. Formed exciting plans to update the store, waiting for the older generation to move over so that she could make it happen,' he said. 'Just what you're doing now, India. Until, like you, she found events overtaking her.'

'I see.' And finally she did see. She'd thought she was the first woman to have fought for her place at the head of the company. Clearly she wasn't. It explained a lot. His antagonism towards her father. The bad feeling between the families.

It didn't explain the kisses...

'I've left a copy of the plans for the alterations on my desk,' she said, changing the subject. 'Why don't you go on up, take a look at them? I'll be right up.' Just as soon as she'd had a moment to collect her thoughts.

'I'll pick up the plans,' he said, 'but then I'll leave you in peace for the rest of the morning.' About to ask him what had happened to the month he was supposed to be devoting exclusively to her, she came to her senses just in time. 'Keep lunchtime free, though.' Not so much an invitation as an order, she thought. Maybe that was the way it was in his world. He spoke and people jumped. Willingly.

'You mean I don't get a shadow-break at lunch?'

'Neither of us do.'

She should have been angry, yet his tone was warm enough for her to give him the benefit of the doubt. And there was the suspicion of a smile in the way his eyes creased at the corners. 'I'll reserve a table in the Roof Garden Restaurant. One o'clock?' she suggested.

'One o'clock will be fine. But I find the store a little...public. I'll ask my secretary to book something and ring you with the details.'

Give him the benefit of the doubt and he'd take advantage every time, she thought. Of her lips. Her hands. Her hair. 'There's no need to put her to so much trouble. I'm happy being in public.'

'On show for your customers?'

The more people around the better, as far as she was concerned. He hadn't kissed her in public. Yet. 'It gives the customers confidence if you eat in your own restaurants, Jordan. The Roof Garden at one.'

And this time she didn't give him the opportunity to contradict her, but stepped onto the escalator and was whisked smoothly away from him.

'For a man who hates publicity, you've had quite a day.' His secretary looked up from the first edition of the *Evening Post* as Jordan hooked his hip onto the corner of her desk, picking up a handful of mail awaiting his attention, flicking through it 'Nice photograph. Pity it isn't for real.'

She turned the paper towards him. The picture of him, Serena and her baby was like a hundred others he'd seen in newspapers over the years. The only difference was that in the others the man in the picture was the baby's father.

'She's rather young for me, don't you think?'

'Don't change the subject. You're thirty-seven. It's time you started putting your talent for funding growth industries into making babies instead of money. What were you doing playing midwife in the nursery department at C&F, anyway?'

'Beating India Claibourne at her own game. She was wandering around playing lady of the manor while I got on with the job.'

'How did she take that?'

Jordan thought about it for a moment, then smiled. 'Her smile was as wide and as genuine as a crocodile's.'

'Oh, shame on you, JD. I've seen photographs. She has a lovely smile.'

'No comment.'

'What's she like? She looks very elegant—very aristocratic in her photographs. But then she has the genes. Her father was quite the handsomest man in London in his day. A real pin-up and quite irresistible. I met him once years ago. The man is utterly charming.'

'He could charm a nun out of her knickers.'

'And her mother was stunning. Exotic.'

'Her father was—probably still is—a philanderer, and her mother abandoned her when she was three months old. But you're right. India Claibourne is lovely.' He found himself thinking about the moment he'd taken her hand, felt it trembling in his. He'd wanted to take her in his arms, hold her, promise her anything…

'JD?'

Christine was regarding him with a dangerously thoughtful expression and he smiled. 'She's clever too. Kitty Farraday mark two,' he said, thinking about his own mother. 'And equally doomed to disappointment.'

'Oh, right. Is that why you took her out to dinner last night? To soften the blow?'

He frowned. 'How do you know I had dinner with India last night?'

She picked up the paper. 'Page seven. City Diary,' she said, then read. '"Is Jordan Farraday going for the hat trick? Will he claim India Claibourne along with the department store that bears both their names, healing the thirty-year-old feud with a personal as well as a business partnership? The ongoing saga of the fight for control at Claibourne & Farraday took another romantic twist last night, when Jordan Farraday and India Claibourne were spotted after hours, dining *à deux* at Giovanni's..."'

'Oh, please! Stop!'

'Yes, well, it's fairly predictable stuff, considering recent events.' She offered him the paper. He declined the pleasure of reading about his supper *'à deux'* with a shake of his head.

'I wonder how the *Post* found out that we dined at Giovanni's? Apart from the two of us, only you knew about it.' He cocked a brow at her. 'You wouldn't be trying to advance your cause in the hope of winning the sweepstake?' He waited. 'The *Post* seems to know all about that, too.'

'You've already read this, haven't you?'

'No. I had a call from *Celebrity* magazine. They quoted it in full, asking me for a comment. My brisk "no comment" only provoked the offer of a stunning amount of money to cover the wedding.'

'Well, don't blame me. The *Post* have probably got a "most wanted" call out on sightings of the two of you together. Take a leaf out of Niall and Bram's book and run away now,' Christine advised, 'before it turns into a media circus.'

'Come on, Christine. I don't need this.'

'No? Well, maybe Miss Claibourne does,' she said. 'It wouldn't hurt her cause to have you appear to be wooing her, would it? It would certainly make everyone think twice before assuming that you were about to take over.'

He'd thought that Christine was having a little fun at his expense. Maybe he was being naïve. He had history as proof of how far the Claibournes would go to take, keep control of the store.

'See what you can find out. Discreetly. I don't want to excite any more interest in this affair.'

'Nice choice of words.' Then, 'You really can't blame the *Post* for running with the story, especially when you're being so co-operative. Giovanni's isn't the first restaurant that leaps to mind when you're considering a working supper. Did she enjoy herself?'

'India? I couldn't say.'

'Then she must be one very cool young woman. Did *you*?' she pressed.

'She's interesting,' he said, non-committally.

'As well as beautiful and clever. An unbeatable combination.'

He got to his feet. 'I have to go. I'm having a working lunch with a beautiful, clever and interesting lady in C&F's rooftop restaurant. The venue is her choice. I'm telling you now so that you can send out for the late edition of the *Post* and read all about it.'

'Did you look at the plans for the top floor?'

Jordan had spent lunch questioning her about the catering arrangements at the store. They had four restaurants, three coffee shops and a sushi bar, and they were always busy. He'd asked intelligent questions—if she had a suspicious nature she'd have to wonder if he'd been advised what questions to ask by someone in the business. He must know people, have provided finance for new restaurants. Celebrity chefs were a growth industry.

Eventually he'd seemed satisfied, and now it was her opportunity to bring up the plans.

'I glanced at them. Your architect appears to have done a good job in a very short time. You did say that Niall put forward the idea?'

She hadn't, but since she didn't know what Niall had told him she had no choice but to allow that a Farraday had had some input. This wasn't the moment to be caught out in a lie.

'He and Romana discussed it, apparently. They were both in a hurry to clean up after some PR event and Niall was shocked at the profligate waste of space—'

'More likely irritated that there was no excuse to share a bathroom.'

She raised her eyebrows. 'Maybe. Whatever the reason, it sometimes takes an outsider to spot the obvious.'

'Niall isn't an outsider. He's a partner.'

'A sleeping one,' she pointed out. Jordan raised an eyebrow back at her. 'He brought a fresh eye to things,' she continued, doing her best to ignore the heat rising to her cheeks. 'Romana wrote a report and e-mailed it to me.'

'From her honeymoon?'

'There,' she said, offering his own words back to him with a wide and generous gesture. 'You *see* how dedicated we are.'

He smiled at that. 'I never doubted it for a moment, India. Or the usefulness of a "fresh eye". This is a beautiful and successful store, but it's rather stagnated under your father's stewardship. A fresh eye is exactly what it needs.'

'And it's got one. Since I became a director,' she said, 'I've been working hard on attracting a more youthful customer base. The trick is not to put off the people who love it just the way it is. Not to startle them.'

'Maybe the younger audience just need a new store.'

'A "Miss" Claibourne & Farraday in every shopping mall?' She pulled a face, yet something chimed in her head. A new dedicated store…

'So what's your vision? Will you share it with me?' he asked, bringing her back to him.

Was he giving her an opportunity to make her case? Prove herself? Seriously? Or did he imagine he would be able to pick it to pieces? Make her look foolish?

She could run the basics by him. Rethinking the use of space. Refreshing the interiors within the confines of the protected listed status. Getting rid of the clutter, opening everything out. Cosmetic changes. But what would he say if she told him that his name was redundant in her plans?

He insisted he was a businessman first and last. Would he see the benefit? Put that above personal recognition? It seemed unlikely.

She certainly wasn't going to tell him without carefully thinking it through. She'd need to know a lot more about Jordan Farraday before she took the risk of telling him that she planned to relaunch the store as Claibourne's.

'I'd be glad to, Jordan, but not right now. Right now I have to negotiate a new contract with the company that provides our laundry services.' She smiled. 'It's not all bikinis and bone china.' She hooked her hair behind her ear, then quickly shook it free before he decided to loosen it for her. 'Maybe we can find some time at the weekend,' she said, summoning the waitress in order to sign the bill. 'To talk?'

'Break the solemn "no business" rule?' he asked, his expression solemn, only his eyes suggesting he was teasing. 'There's a heavy fine for that.'

'Oh, yes. I forgot.' Then, 'But who would know? If we took a walk, say? If we didn't tell them?'

'We'd have to own up. It's an honour system.'

'Of course. It's for charity.' Then, after a moment's thought, 'Actually, you know, if no one breaks the rules there'll be no money to donate. It's almost obligatory, don't you think?'

'Rather more than almost,' he admitted, and he smiled, evidently pleased that she'd so quickly captured the mood of the weekend. 'We'll find some quiet time on Sunday morning.'

Quiet time. A walk through the country with nothing to distract them. It sounded blissful…

'Won't I be expected to peel potatoes, or something, for lunch?'

'For a small fee,' he offered, 'I'll fix the rota.'

'You can do that?' Stupid question. 'In that case,' she said, 'it's a date.' And she felt as breathless, as excited, as scared, as if she was a teenager asked out by the local 'bad boy'.

She knew it was a risk. She knew she shouldn't go. But there wasn't a thing in the world to stop her from saying yes.

The Sales Manager of the laundry service arrived, determined on a substantial rates increase, took one look at

Jordan Farraday, sitting to one side of India's desk, silently observing the discussions, and was suddenly all sweet reason. A meeting that she'd anticipated would take two hours of hard negotiation was over in less than half the time.

'Can I retain your services?' India asked Jordan when the man had gone. 'As a contract negotiator.'

'You seem perfectly capable of negotiating your own contracts.'

'I am. And I'd have got the same deal in the end, because he needs our contract just as much as we need his services. But it was a lot quicker once that guy thought he had to impress you.'

'I didn't say a word,' he protested.

'You didn't have to. You just looked—' she sought an appropriate adjective '—unimpressed. Thanks to the *Evening Post*, it's public knowledge that you're hoping to take over the store. I suspect he wanted to get the contract signed and sealed before that happened. He probably thought he'd have to cut his prices a lot more to impress you.'

'Then he was wrong. The deal was fair; the guy has to make a profit. But don't knock yourself. You do a very fine "unimpressed" yourself. I'm impressed.'

'Thank you,' she said, just a touch wryly.

He matched her smile and doubled it. 'You're welcome.'

She sat back in her chair, just looking at him. It wasn't a hardship. Every woman should have a man like him about the place—a living sculpture—to look at from time to time.

'Why are you here, Jordan?' He made a gesture, asking if she meant 'here' as in sitting in this chair. She shook her head. 'You must have better things to do with your valuable time than watch me negotiate the laundry bill.'

'I can think of worse ways to spend an afternoon.'

'That doesn't answer my question.'

'Maybe I'm just curious. Maybe I just want to see what all the fuss is about. Find out what's the big attraction in running a department store.' Maybe she shouldn't have asked a question she knew he wouldn't give a straight answer to. 'I've done that, so why don't we take the rest of the day off? Go out for the afternoon?'

'Out?' The man could change the subject without taking a pause for breath.

'It's a lovely afternoon, and by your own admission you've saved an hour. And you've got no other appointments for the rest of the day.' Before she could invent something urgent, he added, 'Not according to your diary.'

'You looked at my diary?' she demanded, outraged.

'As if I would. That would have been the worst kind of prying,' he declared, placing his hand on his heart in a gesture that didn't fool her for a minute and adopting an expression that made her want to giggle. 'I checked with Sally this morning, when I picked up the plans. What do you say? We could take a walk in St James's park, feed the ducks, maybe even have an ice-cream.'

The idea of Jordan eating an ice-cream cone was so ridiculous that she very nearly succumbed. But she put on a stern expression and said, 'I'm supposed to be convincing you that I'm a dedicated, hard-working Chief Executive.'

'Well, relax. I'm convinced. In fact I'm sure I've already told you that I'd offer you the job as CEO if I thought for a minute you'd take it. We'd make a great team.'

'With you in control and me taking orders? I don't think so.'

'Why don't we give it a try? Miss Claibourne,' he said firmly, 'take the afternoon off.'

'Mr Farraday,' she replied, 'get lost.'

CHAPTER EIGHT

JORDAN didn't attempt to change her mind. He simply got up, leaned over the desk, and kissed her cheek. 'I'll see you later,' he said, before walking out of her office.

For a moment India sat quite still, stunned by the suddenness of his departure, attempting to unscramble the complex mixture of emotions that surged through her.

She knew what she should be feeling. Ever since he'd walked into her store she'd been wishing him somewhere else. It was pure contrariness to be peeved just because he'd done exactly as she asked, and 'got lost'. To want to know where he was going. What he was doing without her.

And *later*? What did that mean? Was he coming back? Today? Tomorrow?

What was she doing? Putting a brake on the roller-coaster ride her mind was taking, she reminded herself that she had a store to save. And she was running out of time. If she could find out who had written the letter she should be able to work out who'd been the recipient. It hadn't been dated, but the yellowed paper suggested it was older than the rest of the contents of the file. Which begged another question. What had it been doing there?

She'd taken advantage of Jordan's earlier absence to visit her father's new Docklands apartment and go through his desk. She hadn't expected to find the letter, but had hoped for some clue as to his present whereabouts. She'd organised a quiet villa for him in the south of France after his cruise, but he'd stayed there no more than a week, and where he'd gone from there, she had absolutely no idea.

She'd been stunned to find a postcard with a Lahore postmark, reminding his cleaner that he'd loaned his flat to an old friend for a week. Lahore? Pakistan? What on earth was he doing there? And would his heart stand it? She'd put through a call to the Consul, hoping he might have called there. He hadn't.

Now, her second port of call was Maureen Derbyshire. She'd worked in the registry, where the files and records were stored, for fifty years, had run it for the last thirty, and knew every scrap of paper in it. It was possible she'd recognise the handwriting...

Maureen read the note. 'You're looking for this letter? I can tell you now that it's not here.'

No, she hadn't expected it to be that easy—although overlooking the obvious was always a mistake. 'I was hoping you might recognise the handwriting. Or even the notepaper.'

'Not offhand, but I'll look through some of the older files. The legal stuff. I might find a match.' She frowned, then said hesitantly, 'You know, hiding something is all very well, India, but unless someone else knows about it you might as well throw it on the fire.'

'What are you saying?'

'If the letter still existed your father would have told someone. When he was so ill.'

'He didn't tell me about the golden share agreement.'

'Which rather proves my point. You always were his favourite; if he had the letter, or knew where it was, he would have used it. Just as the Farradays would have done thirty years ago, if they'd had it.'

Shaken by the simplicity of the woman's logic, India photocopied the note, then snipped off a piece of the handwriting that gave no clue to its disturbing contents before shredding the rest of the copy. Then she took a sample of the notepaper before returning it.

She wanted to stay. Ask Maureen what had happened when her father took over. Ask her about Kitty Farraday and her dreams. 'I have to go. I'm needed at the main reception desk…'

'Go. Leave this with me. I'll see what I can find.'

'Thank you.'

Despite Maureen's gloomy prognosis, India's step was lighter as she ran up the stairs to the ground floor. She felt happier than she had done for weeks. She didn't know why, just that something had changed. That something inside her had shifted focus. Then, as she hurried through the store, she caught herself glancing over her shoulder and she realised what—or rather who—it was.

Jordan Farraday.

The man had been on her mind for weeks. From the day the *Post* had announced her appointment as Managing Director. Within hours he'd issued a legal challenge, citing the golden share agreement, effectively putting her life on hold.

Since then he'd invaded her every waking thought, coloured her actions. She'd looked at pictures of the man, raided the newspaper libraries, trawled the internet for background. She'd even read his entry in *Who's Who*, for heaven's sake. And then he'd walked into her store, as arrogant a piece of manhood as she'd ever come across.

He'd made her angry, made her want to giggle like a girl, and forced her to confront things she'd hadn't given a second's thought in a long time. And he'd done something no one else had ever done.

He'd made her heart stop with a kiss.

Later? When?

'I'm sorry to disturb you, Miss Claibourne, but according to *him*—' the receptionist gave the waiting courier a look that could have left him in no doubt about who should really be apologising '—you have to sign for this personally.'

India signed his receipt and took the large cardboard envelope. When she saw the sender's name—JD Farraday—all lightness of spirit evaporated.

She'd seen him an hour ago. What could be so important that it required an addressee-only signature? Was it the *coup de grâce*?

She'd told him to get lost. Was he responding with a writ to remove her? Had he just been teasing her, toying with her…?

She tore it open, but the envelope inside was not from any lawyer. Was that better? Or worse? It was heavy cream paper, square—very like the stationery she used for her private correspondence. Her name—India—was handwritten in thick, bold strokes.

She raised the flap with her thumb, her hand shaking. Inside were two tickets to a sell-out concert being given by a sensational young violinist at the Festival Hall that evening.

The note attached said, 'I'll be on the terrace at seven. J.'

Later.

* * *

Jordan leaned on the terrace wall, staring across the river. Seeing nothing. Only wondering if she'd come. Trying to tell himself that this was simply part of his game plan.

It was like fishing. In order to catch your prey, you had to use the right bait. And he'd done his homework. He'd known that India Claibourne was a regular patron of the Festival Hall long before she'd told him so, and the tickets had been bought weeks ago, in the certainty that they'd be worth their weight in gold. Which was considerably less than they'd cost.

He'd known that inviting her out on a date was never going to work. He'd pushed her into dinner last night. He'd found a way to twist her arm into joining him for the weekend. There was no future in that. The lady had to *want* to come—which was why, tonight, he was playing the gentleman, offering her the choice. Having first made it as hard for her to say no as he knew how.

Hard. But not impossible.

With any other woman he'd have put money on her making him wait just long enough for him to wonder whether she wouldn't turn up. Five…seven minutes maximum. No longer, just in case he wasn't a patient man and didn't like being kept waiting.

India wasn't any other woman. She was a match for him, which meant he should have been able to anticipate her response. In fact, it meant her response was never going to be predictable.

He glanced at his watch. She was already ten minutes late. Eleven. He straightened, dragged his hands through his hair, rubbed them over his face, as if somehow he could eradicate the aching spread of regret, rub out the realisation that if she didn't come he'd lost more than a cynical gamble that he could manipulate her…

The thought snagged, caught up on a hot shaft of desire, as he turned and saw her walking towards him.

Tall, exotically dark, stunningly beautiful, in a high-necked jacket cut from heavy silk, its gold embroidery catching the evening sunlight, and softly gathered trousers narrowing into a stitched cuff at the ankle. A vision in burgundy and gold.

He would have put money on it. She wasn't going to miss any opportunity to make that statement.

It didn't matter. She was here. He'd called and she'd come. Whether she knew it or not, he was already in control.

So why didn't it feel like a victory?

'I'm so sorry I'm late,' she said as she joined him. 'I set out in good time but there was an accident by Vauxhall Bridge. I thought the cab driver was going to explode.'

'You're fine.' Much more than fine. As he took her hand, bent to kiss her cheek, he caught the faintest trace of jasmine. She'd matched her scent to her look, and on an impulse he glanced down and saw the delicate tracery of hennaed designs that patterned her hands. He had a momentary, mind-blowing vision of those hands against his skin. 'We've got time for a drink,' he offered, in an effort to divert the thought. Get her into the bustle of the bar. Dilute the impact of her presence in the crowd.

'Do you mind if we don't? I've been inside all day and I'd like the chance to enjoy the fresh air.' He offered his arm without a word, glad that she'd said no. She took it, looping her arm through his, laying her hand on his sleeve and turning to walk with him. 'Did you take your stroll in the park this afternoon?' she asked, glancing up at him, the merest suggestion of suppressed laughter in her eyes. 'How was the ice-cream?'

'Chastened by your puritan work ethic, I went back to my office and did a lot of boring stuff instead.'

The laughter bubbled over. 'You're sure it wasn't just to check out rumours of an office sweepstake on the consummation of a romance between us?'

'You saw the *Post*?' Stupid question. Obviously she'd seen it.

'Required reading,' she assured him. 'You made quite a splash, Jordan. The City Diary, entertaining as it was, was small beer compared to the photograph of you with our celebrity author. And you with Serena, her baby in your arms. What a pity they didn't get you with the chef...' Her pause was majestic. 'Or you'd have made the...um...hat trick.' And she caught her lower lip in her teeth to stop herself from laughing out loud.

There was no point in standing on his dignity—besides, he wanted to see that laugh. 'I expected the photograph of me with the baby,' he said, grinning broadly. 'But did they really have to suggest that I had personally delivered the infant on the nursery department floor?'

'Why would a newspaper spoil a good story by sticking to the truth? And you have to admit it makes the store look good,' she said. 'Very caring.'

'It might make the store look good. But if my mother sees it—' and someone would undoubtedly send it to her '—it will make her broody for grandchildren.' He heard his words, the not-in-this-lifetime sentiment, and found himself for the first time in his life doubting them. He'd had a glimpse of something, holding that infant, watching India cradle her, her expression soft as the tiny fingers had gripped her own—had finally understood the atavistic urge to pass on the genes, seek immortality in a new generation. He felt it now, with India's scent filling his head, the silk whispering against her skin as she walked. She was hidden from him, from everyone. Kept secret. With only her face and her painted hands to hint at the beauty concealed. He'd never seen anything more erotic, more arousing. Perhaps it was as well that they were strolling amidst the arid concrete terraces of the Festival Hall or he might have forgotten himself completely. 'The burden of the only child,' he said.

'At least your mother cares, Jordan.' And as he glanced down at her he saw the sparkle go out of her eyes. 'She never married?'

'No—' He wanted to ask her about *her* mother. Whether she ever saw her. Wanted to know everything. 'I think we'd better go inside.'

India waited while Jordan went to buy a couple of programmes, apparently oblivious of the way women glanced in his direction, then turned to look again with hungry eyes. He'd abandoned the formality of his City chalk-stripe in favour of a cream suit and a dark blue collarless shirt, unbuttoned at the neck. He looked relaxed, at ease with himself and the world. And very definitely good enough to eat.

Dangerously so.

She saw the women look, and, far from oblivious, she felt a choking upsurge of possessiveness. Wanted to tell them to keep their eyes to themselves.

Then, as he took the programmes, he glanced up, caught her gaze and smiled—just for her. An intimate, I'm-glad-you're-here look that made everyone else disappear. Made her feel rare and precious.

She wasn't certain why she'd decided to come. She knew that Jordan thought he was being very clever, giving her an order in a way that she'd find impossible to refuse, and her first response had been to drop the envelope, tickets and all, into the nearest bin.

But then she'd decided that it didn't matter. He might think he was winning, but she knew that if she accepted the challenge, took the risk, then whatever happened in the future—tonight, listening to a concert with someone who shared her passion for music—she couldn't lose.

It was the first time he'd ever been to a concert and found the music less compelling than his companion. India sat so still, so rapt. Once, during a slow *canzonetta*, played with such deeply felt perfection by the young Korean violinist, she reached out blindly and he caught her hand, held it. She glanced at him, apparently startled to discover that he was beside her, and as he watched a tear welled up, spilled over.

He wanted to kiss it from her cheek, taste it. He wanted to taste her, every bit of her, and he wanted to take his time. Take the slow, scenic route via her temple, the hollows of her throat, the corner of her mouth, where he'd noticed a tiny crease that sometimes betrayed the beginnings of a smile.

He wanted to graze the tender place behind her ear. Lift her hair and tease the back of her neck, her shoulders, driving her insane as he made her wait. Made himself wait.

If they'd been alone, this would have been the moment. She was boneless, beyond reason, and that was how he wanted her. Lost to reason. Wanting him so much that nothing else mattered.

The way, as he'd discovered some time during the last forty-eight hours, that he wanted her.

She started as the tempo changed suddenly, turned back to the platform. And he discovered that he'd been holding his breath, hoping that she would leave her hand in his. Just so that he could touch her.

And she did.

'Thank you, Jordan. That was...' India felt unable to express her feelings in words and filled the gap with a gesture that invited him to help her out.

'Yes, it was,' he said, responding to her silent plea. 'Very...' And he copied her gesture, mimicking the helpless little pause.

She laughed. 'Two minds with a single thought.'

'Let's see if we can double it. Are you hungry?'

'Yes.'

'Italian? Japanese? Thai?'

'American,' she said. 'I'd like a hot dog.'

'A hot dog,' he repeated evenly.

'With double onions and plenty of mustard. There's a place by Waterloo Bridge.'

'Well, you're easy to please.'

Not that easy. 'We can eat them as we walk along the Victoria Embankment.'

He glanced at her shoes—soft, low-heeled favourites—

and said, 'Sure. If that's what you want.' *Sure?* That was it? No indulgent laughter? No firm redirection to a 'charming little restaurant that you'll love'? That was the way James had dealt with a similar request on an evening when the music had been sublime and all she'd wanted to do was walk.

Could it be that Jordan Farraday had asked her what she wanted and then offered her the unusual compliment of believing that she meant it?

He was even cleverer than she thought.

They emerged to the mayhem of hundreds of concert-goers trying to connect with pre-booked taxis. 'I'll just tell the driver that there's been a change of plan,' he said, and crossed to a sleek Daimler parked at the kerb to speak briefly to the driver before taking her arm, hooking it under his.

They walked in silence for a while, and normally she would have been glad to have an opportunity to come down from the concert. But tonight the concert had slipped away in that moment she'd turned and seen Jordan watching her. There had been something unguarded in that look. No intent to charm.

The arrogance of a man in control of himself, and everyone around him, had gone, and he'd looked so vulnerable that she'd wanted to take his face in her hands and kiss him. Reassure him. Tell him that everything would be all right. That, together, they could work things out.

Crazy enough, if forgivable in a moment of high emotion.

Yet now, walking at his side, her arm within the encompassing safety of his, she was still, on some subconscious level, aware of everything that he had been feeling in the semi darkness of the concert hall. Could hear his unspoken thoughts, feel the heat of a desire that reached out and warmed her.

'English or French?' They had come to a halt a few yards from the hot dog vendor. She looked up. 'Mustard?'

'Oh, English, please.' she said. His mouth quirked. 'What?'

'I'd have put money on it,' he said, giving the vendor their order, not forgetting the double onions for her. He wrapped her hot dog in a couple of napkins, added the English mustard and handed it to her.

She captured an onion making an escape bid, and popped it in her mouth, sucked the juice from her thumb. 'Are you suggesting that I'm predictable?'

'Anything but predictable. I'm suggesting you're not a woman to take the easy option.'

She bit into her hot dog, then began to walk across the bridge. 'Not a woman to give up and hand over her department store without a fight,' she agreed.

'Forget the store for tonight. I want to hear about you.'

The classic opening move. 'You know all there is to know about me, Jordan. I'm an open book to you. Or should I say an open file of newspaper clippings?'

'Newspaper clippings tell the bare bones of a story. There's no heart in them. Nothing of emotion, or pain, or feeling.' They walked for a while. 'Tell me about your mother.'

He was going for pain, then. 'You probably know as much as I do.' She shrugged, turned and leaned on the bridge parapet. 'She met my father when he was in India, doing that seventies hippie thing. They were happy doing their own thing, being young and irresponsible. Then your grandfather's car skidded on an icy road and real life butted in.' She licked the mustard from her fingers, trying to imagine how that must have affected everyone. Especially Jordan's mother.

Her own father's heart attack had thrown everything into the air, making life difficult enough. But at least he'd recovered sufficiently to worry her that he was overdoing it. *Lahore?* Was he going on some rerun of his youthful past? Whatever he was doing, if he took care of himself he'd live out his allotted span and then some.

But if he'd died what would she and Flora and Romana be feeling now? How would they have coped? Would the loss of the store have even mattered?

'It must have been hard on your mother,' she said, turning to look at him. 'Did she have anyone to turn to?'

'She had her sisters. Niall's mother and Bram's.'

'Of course.'

He shrugged. 'They did what they could, but they were married—one living in Scotland, the other in Norfolk. They had young families.'

'She just had you, then?'

'Eight years old and more trouble than I was worth. She needed more than that.' He shrugged. 'And there was someone. A man with a broad shoulder to weep on.'

'Someone she trusted?'

'Someone she trusted,' he agreed. Then, grimly, 'We all make mistakes.'

'Oh.' She looked down into the river. Dark and deep as family secrets.

'You were telling me about your mother,' Jordan said after a while. 'Pamela? Her mother was Eurasian?'

'You do have a retentive memory.' But, glad to change the subject, deflect his own dark memories, she turned to her own. 'I don't know anything except what other people have told me. She was a happy hippie, expecting her first child, probably indulging herself in flights of fancy about herself as the great earth mother. And maybe it would have worked. If they could have stayed in India, living simply, with no one to please but themselves. But overnight my father stopped doing whatever it was hippies did. Shed the beads, cut his hair, embracing establishment mores and marrying my pregnant mother in the nick of respectability.' Not such a huge change for him; he'd just been returning to what he knew. For her mother—leaving the sun, the light, the freedom, for cold, wet London and a mother-in-law who had undoubtedly been as cold as the weather—it had to have been a nightmare. She sighed. 'Before assuming his rightful place as head of Claibourne & Farraday.'

'You admit it was his rightful place?'

The switch was so quick that she nearly missed it. Nearly said the words he wanted to hear. Because her agreement would justify his own claim.

'A question to which any answer would be wrong,' she said, once her brain had scrambled back to reality. She glanced at him sideways. He'd finished his hot dog, balled the paper napkin and stuffed it into his pocket. 'You'll be sorry for that when you open your wardrobe tomorrow.'

'I'm already sorry. Do you do this often?'

'Not often,' she admitted. 'Not many men are as indulgent as you.' As unexpectedly romantic. Or did she mean cynically romantic? An indulgent man was a man who wanted something.

'Are you telling me that this culinary nightmare was in the nature of a tease?' He grinned. 'If that's the case, Indie, you're in trouble. The car is waiting for us in Westminster, at the far end of the Victoria Embankment, and all the money in the world isn't going to find us a cruising taxi at this time of night.'

Indie? Her sisters and her friends used the diminutive. It was familiar, warm. But when Jordan Farraday said it he added a whole new intimacy to the word, his voice layering on texture, depth of meaning. Making it sound brand-new. She took her time about finishing her hot dog before she said, 'I wasn't teasing.'

'No?' He took her napkin from her, hooked his finger and thumb beneath her chin and turned her to the light. For a moment she thought she must have a trace of mustard on her lip, that he was going to wipe it away. But he just stood there, looking down at her. 'What were you doing, India?'

Following her heart rather than her head. Stretching the evening out, not wanting it to ever end...

It had still been quite light when they'd left the Festival Hall, but the darkness had closed in as they walked. Now the lights were shining on the river. It was a magical scene, and she was about to be kissed by a man whose agenda involved taking her life away from her.

While she aided and abetted him by falling in love with him. Fooling herself that he was falling in love with her.

What would he do if he knew that?

There was only one way to find out. Give him the green light.

'What I'm doing, Jordan Farraday, is repaying you for a wonderful evening by taking the most wicked advantage of you,' she said, the shake in her voice as she put her heart on the line barely noticeable. 'I like to walk by the river at night, but I couldn't do this on my own.' She lowered her lashes, then raised them again swiftly, to look up at him like the very worst kind of flirt. 'Do you mind, darling?'

He stiffened. His hand dropped to his side.

'Not at all,' he said, the ragged softness gone from his voice. 'A walk in the evening before bed clears the head, I find.'

He stood aside so that she could turn and walk. It was like moving away from the fire on a cold night. For a moment she didn't move, stunned at the sudden change in him. He'd reacted as if she'd slapped him, his expression one of shock at her blatant come-and-get-me look. A cynic wouldn't have picked up the false note she'd deliberately injected into her response; he'd have been waiting for that invitation, expecting it. He wouldn't have been repelled by her blatant come-on.

Oh, dear God. She had it wrong. Whatever else had been going on between them, tonight he hadn't been pretending. Stop the world! Rewind the tape to that moment before she'd spoken.

But life didn't do reruns. There was no second chance. She'd been the cynic, believing the worst of him instead of hoping for the best. For Romana, for Flora, romancing their Farradays had offered the happy-ever-after ending. But she didn't believe in fairy tales. She'd put Jordan's sincerity to the test and now she had to live with the result.

She forced her feet to move, begin walking, and he fell in beside her. But he didn't take her arm again.

As she walked, a full six inches of space between them, her feet, which had been so light until a moment ago, were now leaden. And, a little below her left breast, her heart felt much the same way.

CHAPTER NINE

JORDAN felt empty. Hollow. He was supposed to be in control of this. He was the one who was going to walk away unscathed with India Claibourne's heart, her body and her department store, leaving her suffering all the pain and humiliation that his mother had gone through thirty years earlier.

That was the plan and it had been going so well.

She'd come when he'd called—she'd kept him waiting, but she'd come. Moved by a moment of high emotion, she'd reached out for his hand in the darkness of the concert hall. She'd been playful when he'd invited her to supper, and the slow, romantic walk along the embankment had been her suggestion.

It couldn't have been going better if he'd written the script in advance. So how come he'd been so angry when she'd put on that coquettish, eyelash-flapping little display? As clear an invitation to end the evening in her bed as a man could get.

Was it the fact that she was so obviously pretending that had so angered him? That she was prepared to do anything to save her precious store?

Wasn't that what he wanted?

India Claibourne that desperate?

He no longer had an answer. Only the certainty that he wanted India Claibourne. Wanted her in his arms, her skin against his, wanted her whimpering softly as he possessed her, wanted him to forget everything but him.

For a moment before she'd gone for straight cynicism he'd seen something else in the depths of her lovely eyes, something artless and pure and sincere that had made him feel brand-new, reborn.

In that moment he'd known that he wanted her as he'd wanted no other woman. His. For ever.

But not in exchange for a department store.

'What did your mother do?' They'd been walking in silence for what seemed like for ever. Not touching. Not speaking. The air between them was as solid as a brick wall. One with a decorative topping of razor wire. India couldn't bear it. 'Afterwards?' she persisted. India sensed that he'd turned to look at her, but she knew instinctively that it would be a mistake to turn and confront his frosty gaze. That keeping her eyes directed at some indefinable point in the distance was the only way to hold his attention. 'After my father took over?' The silence went on so long that she finally gave in, looked up at him. 'You said—'

He looked away. 'I know what I said.'

His words, his tone, did nothing to encourage her. But he had answered…

'Dreamed dreams, you said.' He acknowledged her words with the slightest movement of his head. Kept walking.

It felt like pushing treacle uphill, but she wouldn't let it go.

Somehow what had happened to his mother was tied up with what was happening now, and no one was telling her the truth. Her father had taken off on some pilgrimage to his youth. The lawyers were going through the motions, but she suspected they had little confidence that the equal opportunity legislation would make a difference. They were just waiting for her to come to terms with reality and accept the inevitable.

Not this side of hell freezing over.

'She dreamed dreams and watched the swinging sixties passing C&F by.' She said it as if she was talking to herself. 'But what did she do *afterwards*?'

'After her dreams were taken from her?' His voice was still cold enough to freeze water. But he kept talking. 'Nothing very much for a long time. She had a breakdown.'

'A breakdown? Oh, Jordan…' She stopped. For a moment he kept walking, then he too stopped.

'What?' he said, his shoulders rigid, his voice sharply impatient. She said nothing and finally he turned, his bitten-down expression betraying the deep-seated pain, the anger he had kept well hidden beneath an urbane, assured façade.

She wanted to go to him, put her arms around him, hold him and make the pain go away. Tell him to let the anger go before it burned him up, ate him from the inside out. But the space between them was a force field of negative emotions keeping her at a distance. Words were the only bridge she had.

'I'm so sorry.' Inadequate words. Useless words. 'I know how devastating grief can be—'

'Grief?' His head went up. 'You think it was simply grief?'

'No. No, of course not.' Not just grief. But grief complicated by guilt might just be enough to tip someone over the edge. And there were always feelings of guilt when someone died suddenly. The nagging memory of harsh words that could never be taken back. And there would undoubtedly have been harsh words about her fatherless offspring. Her guilt would have been compounded by the knowledge that she'd let down a much-loved father. Caused him pain. Then to have had him die like that, with things left unsaid, no chance for forgiveness, to say thank you for the good stuff. To say I love you.

And not just guilt for her. There must have been guilt for Jordan, too, believing he'd been the cause of her pain.

And she shivered.

'Oh, here. You're cold.' He slipped off his jacket, walked back to her and put it round her shoulders, settling it around her, enveloping her in the warmth from his own body. He held the jacket edges for a moment, his gaze fixed on something of intense interest at his feet. Then he took a breath, looked up, met her gaze head-on, and without warning the brick wall crumbled. 'Shall we take the last twenty minutes from the top?' he said. 'Try it again without rattling the skeletons in the Claibourne & Farraday closet?'

Skeletons? What skeletons?

No, she wasn't going to ask. She had to know, but not tonight. They'd reclaimed tonight—done the impossible and set the clock back—and she was saying nothing to risk fracturing their fragile truce. It was enough to have confirmation that there was *something*. Enough to have him smiling at her.

Definitely no skeletons. She scanned her brain for some neutral subject. Something safe. Something that would bring the smile back to his eyes. Cricket? That had to be safe, didn't it? And, coming from her, there was no chance he'd take it seriously. She cleared her throat a little self-consciously and said, 'So...what do you think of England's chances in the Test Match?'

The corner of his mouth lifted promisingly and it was as if he'd turned on her own personal central heating system, all her senses warming in response to him. It was going to be all right. All right.

'Would that be the Lord's Test?'

'There's more than one?' she asked, betraying her total ignorance of the game. Well, she'd wanted him laughing. Wanted to distract him from the memories that haunted him. 'Damn it, Jordan, it was that or the weather, and I thought you might find cricket marginally more interesting. Help me out here.'

'I'll do better than that. I'll take you. To Lord's.'

'Will you?' She tried to sound enthusiastic, but didn't that mean six days on a hard wooden seat? 'Aren't tickets terribly hard to get?' she replied unenthusiastically. 'I wouldn't want to deprive a real fan—'

He threw back his head and laughed. 'I'll take that as a no, shall I?' he said, putting his arm around her shoulders, tucking her in close to him beneath his arm. It was a good place to be.

'I'm sorry. I thought cricket would be safe.'

'We don't have to talk.'

'No.'

And rather more slowly they continued their stroll along the embankment, this time in a silence that wasn't awkward or difficult. Just peaceful. Far too soon they reached Westminster Pier and the waiting Daimler.

He had a word with the driver, then opened the door for her. She slid across the seat and he joined her in the back. 'Thank you for tonight, Jordan. The concert was wonderful. I wouldn't have missed it for anything.'

'I did rather gamble that the prospect of hearing the performance might outweigh the downside of the company you'd be forced to keep.'

'The company was—' she waggled her free hand '—okay.' But her smile was meant to tell him that she'd found his company very special. At least she hoped it did. Then, because she had to say something about what happened on the bridge, 'I just wish—'

'Shh…' He took her hand, raised it briefly to his lips. 'I know.' Then he held it on the seat between them as the car sped towards her Chelsea apartment.

He saw her to her door. Waited while she opened it and switched off the alarm. She slipped off his jacket before turning to him with it. He was leaning against the doorframe, watching her from beneath heavy-lidded eyes. It was a look that brought her whole body to urgent, demanding life.

He was right about it being too long, but that wasn't why she wanted to grab his shirt and drag him inside. Kiss him stupid, the way he'd kissed her, before taking him to her bed and staying there for a week.

What she was feeling went way beyond sexual attraction. That was simply the physical manifestation of an emotional pair-bonding. Jordan Farraday had been on her mind, day and night, for more than two months. Filling her thoughts, driving her actions. She was as familiar with his photograph as she was with her own face in the mirror. Every day she'd looked at it and asked herself what it would take to get him off her back.

But she didn't want him off her back any more. She just wanted him. In her life, in her heart—

She'd known the truth from the moment she'd first set eyes on the real flesh and blood Jordan Farraday. It had been like an electrical charge. Switching her on. Lighting her up. Watching him hold that girl's hand, she'd known without doubt that under similar circumstances she'd want him at her side. No one else. Holding her hand. Never letting go.

He might be arrogant, but his was the arrogance of strength. He knew his worth. And, like all truly strong men, he knew how to be tender.

In that moment she'd recognised her perfect partner. Her soul mate. She would never meet another man like him, and she was afraid that if they didn't take the moment, right now, then this stupid, pointless dispute would come between them and something that could have been truly special would be lost for ever.

She'd come close to throwing it away tonight, on Waterloo Bridge, in a rush of certainty that all the charm, all the charged looks, were nothing but a cynical attempt to turn her head, seduce her out of the store. She'd turned the tables, switching him off with her less than subtle temptress routine—letting him know that she wasn't fooled when all she'd really wanted to do was turn him on.

And still she didn't really know whether, for him, this was all a game. Whether he'd been truly shocked by her performance, or whether he'd caught on to the fact that he'd have to play it much cooler.

She wasn't even sure if she cared.

She reached up, hooked her hair behind her ear. 'Would you like to come in—?'

His finger touched her lips, stopping the words. Then, with her face cradled in his hand, he kissed her forehead before taking his jacket, turning abruptly and walking swiftly away down the hall to the lift.

'—for a cup of coffee?' she completed, talking to herself.

She shut the door, and leaned against it. Who was she kidding?

He'd seen what she wanted in her eyes. Stopped her before she did something she'd regret, more than anything, for the rest of her life. Except not doing it.

A long peal on the doorbell made her jump. He'd changed his mind…come back…

She fumbled with the catch, hands shaking, and threw back the door—

'India, darling, where have you *been*? I haven't got a tea-leaf to my name.'

It took a moment for the reality, the heart-wrenching disappointment, to sink in. The kind of disappointment that stripped away all pretence and left the heart naked. She wanted Jordan Farraday more than she wanted Claibourne's. True.

Then, still hanging onto the door with one hand, she waved her other in the direction of the kitchen. 'Help yourself, George. Take whatever you want…'

He was almost passed her when he stopped, turned to take a second look. 'India?' She was leaning against the door because if she let it go she'd crumple up on the floor. 'Hey, babe, what's up?'

'Nothing.' But the tears welling up and running unchecked down her cheek betrayed her. 'Everything,' she admitted.

He detached her gently from the life support of the door, holding her as he pushed it shut. 'Want to tell me about it?'

What was there to tell? She'd fallen in love with the wrong man. A man common sense told her was the last man she should ever get involved with. A man her heart was telling her was the only man in the world for her. 'I don't want to want him, George,' she said.

'Who?' He produced a handkerchief.

She ignored it. 'It doesn't matter who,' she said, with a long shuddering sigh. 'I can't have him.'

'I assume we're talking about Jordan Farraday?' He shrugged apologetically when she looked up from his shoulder. 'I read the papers, sweetie. I thought maybe it was going to be wedding number three—'

Which was when she turned into his arms and, for the first time since her pet rabbit had died when she was eight years old, sobbed her heart out.

It was getting to be a habit. Walking away from India's apartment when staying seemed like such a great idea. Shaking with a desire so intense that he felt weak. He leaned against the gleaming roof of the car for a moment, taking deep breaths.

The driver got out. 'Are you okay, Mr Farraday?'

'Just suffering from a bad dose of mixing business with pleasure, Bryan.' He straightened, stepped back, clamped his jaw tight for a moment. 'I'll get over it.'

'Yes, sir.' He opened the car door for him. 'Eaton Square, is it?'

At least he didn't have to drive tonight. He could sit in the back and congratulate himself that his plan was working better than he could have imagined in his wildest dreams.

Tell himself that he would have his revenge on the Claibournes and walk away happy.

Yeah, right.

If everything was so great, why was feeling as if he'd just torn his heart out and left it in India Claibourne's beautiful hands?

He'd seen hot desire in her eyes tonight, a longing that seemed to chime with everything he was feeling. There had been real desire in her eyes in that moment before she'd transformed herself into something else. Something way too calculating. It had brought him up cold.

Maybe, just now, it had been real. But that was the problem. He'd never know whether it was him she wanted, or his surrender. It shouldn't matter. If he was going to break her heart, why would it matter?

But it did.

He looked up at the penthouse windows. Then, before he lost it completely, went back up there, gave away his heart and everything else he had to offer, he said, 'No, Bryan. I need to get out of London tonight.' His Eaton Square apartment was nowhere near far enough away from temptation. 'Take me home.'

George made a great listener. He didn't interrupt. He didn't ask questions. He simply let her hiccup the whole story out in her own way.

'So you see, it's all a mess. He doesn't want me.' He looked doubtful. 'Tonight... I would have... Wanted to...' She sniffed, rubbed her hands over her wet cheeks. 'All he wants is the store.'

'Then give it to him.'

'Claibourne & Farraday?'

'He's going to take it from you anyway, unless you can find this letter, so what's the big deal? If you hand it over, it's your decision. You're in charge. Walk away and he might realise that some things are more important than a fancy emporium with your name over the door.'

'And if he doesn't?'

'Life doesn't come with guarantees, babe. You have to decide what's important to you, what you can't live without. I may just be an old romantic, but I'd always put people before property. Jordan Farraday is unique. Let's face it, you can always open another store.'

Jordan didn't sleep. He spent the night in the book-lined study of the Berkshire manor house that was the family home, the room that had once been his grandfather's private haven, going through the cuttings files. Looking for something...anything... He didn't know what, exactly. Just something to explain why he was so obsessed with India Claibourne.

It was Peter Claibourne he wanted to hurt...but she was the one who haunted his dreams.

There were streaks of light in the sky when he opened the page at a photograph of her that had appeared in a society magazine on her eighteenth birthday. An almost identical photograph of his mother stood on the desk in front of him in an antique silver frame. The debutante 'frock'...the mandatory row of pearls at the throat.

He looked for a long time at the photograph of India, stunningly beautiful, poised on the brink of womanhood. He thought about her eyes that flashed and sparkled with challenge or defiance one moment, then were soft as a puppy's the next. Her mouth...her sweet, hot mouth that drove everything from his mind but her.

And as his fingers moved by themselves to outline her hair, as if to tuck it behind her ear, everything fell into place.

India Claibourne. She'd been there, under his skin, for as long as he could remember. A constant reminder of what his mother had suffered. An irritant that sometimes faded but could never quite be forgotten.

A thorn so deeply embedded in his flesh that it could never be plucked out.

'I'd given up on you,' Sally said, when she came back from lunch and found India working at her desk. 'You and JD Farraday,' she added pointedly.

India, distracted from what she was doing, glanced up from her laptop. 'I worked most of the night. Since we've got Maureen's party tonight, I thought I'd better catch up on some sleep before I came in.'

'Alone?'

'I worked alone and I slept alone.'

'Are you telling me that rumours of a hot romance are entirely without foundation?' She dropped the first edition of the *Post* on her desk. 'The moonlit walk along the embankment was, what? Nothing more than a shortage of taxis?'

India grabbed the paper, read the diary column and groaned. 'Who is doing this to me?'

'Maybe it's him they're doing it to.'

'Well, not any more. It's over.'

'Over?' Sally dropped into a chair, propped her elbows on the desk, her chin in her hands. 'As in over? He's thrown in the towel? Admitted you're better at this than he could ever be?'

'Not that I've heard. No, I've made some decisions of my own. About the future. Since they'll affect you, too, I want you to know exactly what I'm doing before the rumours start flying about.'

And she turned the laptop so that Sally could see the screen, waiting while her secretary scrolled slowly down the proposal she had spent all night putting together.

'You're surrendering the store in return for permission to use the name "India Claibourne" as your own company name, and the "C" product range,' she said at last. 'Is that right?'

'I've spent years trying to get young people through the doors of C&F. Last night it was as if a veil had fallen. This isn't the place for them.' Something Jordan had said had finally clicked into place. 'I'm going to open my own store. Young designers, new labels. What do you think?'

'And what happened to the "over my dead body" declaration?'

'I'm accepting reality, Sally. If I have to give up the store, I want to do it on my own terms.'

'If?'

'When,' she corrected. '*When* I have to give up the store.' She'd had a double whammy this morning. 'I spoke to the lawyers this morning. Counsel's opinion is that my equal opportunities argument will not impress the courts. Treated equally—in other words, taking any question of gender out of the equation—it comes down to age. Jordan has an eight-year head start on me.'

And her call to Maureen, a last ditch hope that she might have found a match for the handwriting or notepaper, had proved fruitless.

The letter—if it existed—would have put them on an equal footing, but the truth was that it no longer mattered. George had said it last night. She could always open another store. She wasn't going to allow this one to stand between her and Jordan.

'You're in love with him,' Sally said, not unsympathetically. 'He's knocked you sideways with dinner at Giovanni's, a bunch of kittens, stolen kisses on the back stairs—'

'Someone saw us…?' Who was she kidding? Of course someone would have seen… 'Is there nothing I've done in the last few days that hasn't been in the *Post*?'

'Only you can answer that.' Then, 'You know this is what he wants, don't you? That he's romancing you right out of the front door? He's got your little hormones so excited that you can't think straight.'

'Just print that out for me, Sally. And fax it to the lawyers with a covering note this afternoon. I want this settled. Finished.' Then maybe there could be a new beginning.

Jordan had been held up in traffic and he was late for Maureen's farewell party. Everyone else had arrived, and he paused in the doorway of the Roof Garden Restaurant looking for India. The crowd shifted, parted briefly, and he caught a glimpse of her, her back to him, talking to a group of people. Caught a glimpse. Caught his breath.

India was dressed to kill. Or at least to cause grievous bodily harm. And her chosen weapon was a slender, close-fitting dress with no visible means of support. The kind of dress that giftwrapped a woman. Made a man believe it was his birthday and Christmas all rolled into one.

Her jet hair, gifted from her mother's gene pool, swung in a sharp, glossy bob. Her jewellery—a choker and wrist-cuffs of gold wire—made her look like a queen. And so she was. Holding court in her kingdom.

Listening intently to one of her guests, she hadn't noticed his arrival, but as the crowds parted for him her companions did and conversation died. Into the void he said, 'I've got a complaint, India. You've got me here under false pretences.'

India, warned by the sudden shift of attention, knew Jordan was at her back the second before he spoke. And every cell in her body lifted a little. Became lighter.

She'd been avoiding the door to the restaurant. She'd spent the first fifteen minutes after she'd arrived looking round every time someone entered, then, catching Sally's pitying look, she'd turned her back on it and concentrated on her guests.

Now, as she turned, looked up, her mouth dried and she could say nothing.

'I was promised the first dance by the Managing Director,' he continued, addressing the entire group. 'But there doesn't appear to be a dance floor.'

'Looks can be deceiving,' Sally said, abandoning her boyfriend at the first sign of fun in order to join them.

'We're dancing outside on the terrace, since it's such a lovely night. Of course you might prefer to take Indie on to a club. Just so that the *Post* has something to write about tomorrow.'

There was an awkward pause that lasted seemingly endless seconds. Then India finally found her voice. 'Maureen, may I introduce Jordan Farraday? The last time you met he couldn't have been more than eight years old—' Then, 'Will you excuse me? The catering manager is trying to attract my attention.' And, leaving Jordan snared by the woman's reminiscences about his boyhood scrapes, she made her escape. Hoping that he'd follow.

Having dealt with a minor query, she circulated, talking to staff, trying not to think about this being the last time they'd all be together. Telling herself that it was not the end, but a new start. Trying to prevent her gaze from drifting towards Jordan, his tall figure dominating the room, to force herself to concentrate, respond coherently to endless questions about her father's health.

She must have succeeded pretty well, because she nearly jumped out of her skin as he put his hand on her shoulder—skin on skin—and leaned across her to shake hands with someone and introduce himself.

It had been a self-protective device—not a particularly successful one—trying to convince herself that he wouldn't come. She'd conceded the store, asked for little in return. But he didn't have to give it to her. Claibourne was a trademarked name… As from today, it was his trademark. And if he was as cynical as Sally had suggested, why would he waste his valuable time on a retirement party?

He moved her on, his hand on her shoulder. 'How was your day?'

'Peaceful without you,' she said, a throwaway line that would have elicited a disbelieving grunt from her secretary. 'How was yours?'

He turned to block out the room. 'Empty. I missed you.' It was a small, still moment before someone demanded her attention. He moved on, easy in company, smiling without strain, chatting easily with anyone and everyone as if nothing had happened. And nothing had. She mustn't read too much into his words. Yet his hand never left her shoulder. His arm remained possessively across her back as they worked the room. And he politely but firmly ejected the store manager from the seat at her side when they sat down to supper.

Their meal was slow and leisurely. It was punctuated with anecdotes about Maureen, short speeches from colleagues and from India. She was eating, she was talking, but she was performing on automatic pilot.

He'd missed her?

'How soon before we can get away?' he asked, as people began to drift out to the terrace.

We? 'If you leave before the dance you've made such a fuss about,' she said, taking nothing for granted, 'Sally will lynch you.'

'Why? Is she planning to take photographs and sell them to *Celebrity*?'

'There's no need. They've sent a staff photographer to cover the event. And you shall have your dance. But not the first dance. *Noblesse oblige*, Jordan. Your first duty tonight is to Maureen.'

'Of course it is. But make no mistake. The last dance

is mine.' He didn't wait for her answer, but took Maureen by the hand. Soon everyone had joined in. India danced with Maureen's husband, with long-serving employees, with shy juniors. Jordan needed no bidding to do the same.

Then she lost sight of him for a moment, turned round in a moment of panic and found herself in his arms, his hand at her back, her hand caught between them, pressed against his chest as he held her close, his cheek against her hair. They didn't so much move as sway in time to the music. 'You were right,' he said, after a moment.

'Right? What's this? Flattery?' Laughter gurgled from her throat. 'I warn you, sir, I'm not used to it. It will go straight to my head.'

'If I'd danced with you first I'd never have been able to let you go.' He stopped and she looked up.

'We can't—'

'This is the last dance, India. We go now, or I kiss you right here—and *Celebrity* magazine will have a lot more than a retirement party to report on.'

CHAPTER TEN

INDIA didn't argue. Neither of them spoke until they were in his car, heading west. As they joined the motorway she turned to him. 'Where are we going?'

'Home.'

His home. She smiled. 'Would that be the Berkshire manor house with its own cricket pitch and a heated pool?' She'd done a little background checking of her own.

'I can't wait until the weekend,' he said, smiling back, not denying it. 'And I'm damn sure I don't want to share you with two randy cricket teams. I want you all to myself.'

He glanced at her, offering her the opportunity to object.

India didn't say a word, and after a while he slowed to turn between the tall brick pillars. The paved drive ran for half a mile or so between an avenue of ancient trees until they turned into the courtyard of a spreading Tudor manor house, with narrow rose-coloured bricks and centuries-old timbering, that lay beneath the moonlight, still and perfect.

'When, exactly, were you going to tell me that this is your house?'

'Technically it's not. My mother inherited it from her father. In reality she's rarely here these days and I take care of everything.'

'I don't suppose she's here now,' she said, and heard her voice catch in her throat.

'She wasn't here this afternoon when I left for London,' he admitted. 'In fact I'm not sure where she is right now. Her last e-mail was from the Afghan border, where she was trying to cross with an aid team.' He almost smiled. 'You did ask what she did...after.'

Charity work. Not the garden party and gala ball fund-raising kind, but hands-on, at the hurting end. 'You must worry about her.'

'Yes, but I try not to let it show too much. It makes her irritable.'

'I'd like to meet her.'

'You will,' he promised.

'And we have twenty-four hours before the cricket teams descend *en masse*?'

'Actually...they're not coming. The weather forecast was for rain, so I postponed it until next month.' She said nothing, just looked up wordlessly at the cloudless sky. 'It's unseasonably warm. I guarantee there'll be thunder by Saturday.'

'It will serve you right if it pours with rain in July,' she said, releasing the seat belt, pushing open the car door and swinging her feet onto the ancient brick paving before standing and, making a big effort not to smile, turning to face him.

He got out of the low sports car, but kept it between them. 'If you're here, I don't care.' His voice was soft as cobweb; his eyes were on fire. Oh, God, he could melt her with a look like that. When she didn't answer, he took his jacket from the back of the car, hooked it over his shoulder and rounded the car to take her hand. 'Come on, this way.' And he turned his back on the house, led the way down a wide brick path, softly illuminated at ground level.

'Where are we going?'

'To take a little walk—clear our heads before bedtime.'

'I'm not sure I want my head *that* clear.' She'd done her thinking, cleared the decks. Now all she wanted was to be in his arms—wanted everything that his eyes were promising.

'We have to talk. About what's going to happen to the store. About the past.'

'We have no past, Jordan.' Maybe, if they were wiser than their forebears, they might have a future. 'The lawyers have my proposal. Leave it to them to thrash out the fine print,' she said as they descended a series of wide, shallow steps. 'As for tonight.' She stopped, looked up at him. 'Tonight, I absolutely forbid shop talk.' Then, as their movement triggered lights in a huge weeping willow, she saw the river, a pretty two-storey boathouse and a wooden jetty. 'I hadn't realised we were so close to the river,' she said, and, retrieving her hand, pulled off her shoes before walking to the end of the jetty, where she sat down, her toes hanging over the edge. 'Oh, swizz, they don't reach the water,' she said, peering down at the inky depths.

'It's been a dry spring.' He draped his jacket over her shoulders and sat beside her.

'Okay, we've done cricket and we've done the weather—'

'India—'

But she didn't want to talk. Talking got them into all kinds of trouble. They hadn't come to this beautiful place to talk. She'd wiped away the past. Was going to build her own future. She hoped that Jordan would be there too, but she didn't want to talk about it. Not right at this minute. And as she turned to look at him she gave a little gasp. 'Stop!' she whispered fiercely.

'What?'

She reached up, laid her hand on his cheek. 'Keep very still—' With her other hand she captured his neck. 'Can you feel it?' she whispered. The feeling that was racing through her, taking control, old as time…

'India…' he warned. 'Wait—'

'I've been waiting for you all my life,' she said, and this time she didn't wait for him to kiss her, but took the initiative, touching his lips with her own. Tempting him softly, tenderly with her tongue. 'Do you feel it, Jordan?' she whispered into his mouth. And she kept him her willing captive as she lay back against the timber jetty, his jacket warm beneath her. For a moment everything was still as he looked down at her, touched her face, her throat, as his fingers outlined the contour of her shoulder.

Then his fingers found the zip at the side of her dress and there was a rush of cool air against her breasts.

Jordan was lost. All his life he'd been the one in control, but India Claibourne could render him helpless with a look, a touch. Somewhere, reason was urging him to stop this now. Tell her everything.

But reason didn't stand a chance, and he pushed down the heavy silk of her dress, lost in wonder as she lay back against the jetty, offering herself to him. Lost in awe as he covered her left breast with the palm of his hand and felt her heart beating, felt her tremble with a desire that echoed his own urgent need.

'I feel it,' he whispered. 'I felt it the first moment I saw you. It was like being plugged into an electric socket.

Switched on.' And his mouth brushed against her temple, teased softly against her cheek, the corner of her mouth.

'Exciting…' she murmured as his mouth sought out the tender spot beneath her ear, teased against her temple, her cheek. 'But terrifying…'

'Like stepping off a cliff…' He heard a sound, a groan, as he kissed her throat, the satin skin of her shoulders, taking the slow, sweet journey that his mind had promised him as they'd sat in the concert hall. He realised that the sound came from somewhere deep inside him.

He'd intended to make things right, to explain what he'd done, before things ever got this far. That was why he'd stayed outside, in the open air, fighting the desperate longing to take her inside, get her into his bed and hang the consequences. It had been the only way he could think of to delay the conflagration until he'd told her the truth. To place the envelope burning a hole in his pocket into her hands before baring his soul. Offering her the only explanation there was, before allowing her to open it. Only afterwards, when he'd seen her reaction, would he have known.

He was wrong about that.

He knew. And for some things there was a perfect moment. While he'd been torturing himself with a conscience as black as sin, India had gone with her instincts. She'd seized that moment. And now he was out of time.

But, as lost to reason as he was, he still wasn't about to make love to her on a floodlit jetty. She complained as he tore himself away. 'We can't stay here, Indie…'

'It's nice out here.'

'We're disturbing the ducks.'

'Oh, hardly. Have you seen the way ducks behave?'

She began to unbutton his shirt. 'And in Royal parks, too...'

'Disgraceful,' he agreed, but he captured her busy hands and as he stood up pulled her to her feet. Her dress slithered to the floor, leaving her wearing nothing but a scrap of lace about her hips, the gold at her throat and wrists. And for once in his life he was utterly lost for words. He just wanted to fall to his knees, offer her his life...

India woke to a perfect gold and blue dawn filtering through the tiny leaded panes of the bedroom window and smiled. She was happy. It was an extraordinary feeling. For months her life had seemed to hover on the brink of disaster. And then, when disaster had finally happened, when she'd surrendered everything, lost everything—she'd discovered that she'd won far more.

She turned to Jordan's supine body and for a while just took pleasure from watching the slow rise and fall of his breathing. Imprinting for ever on her mind the pattern of dark hair that spattered his chest, the sinewy muscles of his arms, the smooth, tempting plane of his stomach. She propped herself on her elbow, leaned over and kissed the hollow beneath his ribs. Nothing happened, but she persisted, curling her tongue round his navel, trailing moist kisses into the hollows of his pelvis.

The response was promising. Encouraged, she continued. Long after it was obvious that Jordan David Farraday was wide awake.

'Are you just going to lie there?' she said after a while, lifting her head to look up at him. 'Leave me to do all the work?'

He folded his arms behind his head and grinned down at her. 'I thought you wanted to be in control.'

She nipped him gently with her teeth and he growled with pleasure. 'What I want is a bit of equality around here.'

He sat up in one fluid movement and caught her arms, drawing her up against him. 'You've got it, Indie.' He looked down into her face. 'All the equality you can handle.'

The mood had shifted, altered to something deeper. 'Show me,' she whispered.

A long time afterwards, with their hair damp from the shower and wrapped only in toweling robes, they went in search of breakfast. But at the top of the stairs Jordan came to a halt and turned to India, taking her hands in his. 'Indie, there's some stuff I have to tell you. Explain. I'd intended to get it all out of the way last night, before—'

'Before I got impatient and jumped you?' Her expression was deadpan.

'Yeah, right,' he said. He could do deadpan. 'I should have listened to my secretary. She warned me about you, India Claibourne. She was sure you were going to use your seductive powers to lure me up the aisle in order keep Claibourne & Farraday all to yourself.'

'I'd have had to be pretty stupid to think I could get away with that.' She lifted one exquisite brow. 'Unless you wanted to be seduced?' He couldn't deny it. He hadn't put up much of a fight... 'After what happened to Niall and Bram you would surely have been on your guard.'

'It wouldn't have helped, apparently. She believes

you're all witches.' He took a damp strand of hair that was clinging to her cheek and tucked it behind her ear. 'I'm inclined to agree with her.'

'Oh, charming,' she said. 'Let me tell you, if we were witches we wouldn't have had to seduce you out of anything. We could have turned you all into frogs—' she clicked her fingers '—just like that.' And, taking hold of the lapels of his robe, she pulled herself up onto her toes and kissed him, hard and sweet. 'Better be careful, Mr Farraday. I still might.' She laughed, her face lighting up, making the National Grid redundant. 'Heavens, you can't know how wonderful I feel.'

'Well, thank you, ma'am. It's good to know one's efforts are truly appreciated—'

She lifted her hand to his cheek. 'Your efforts, my love, were life-altering. Nothing will ever be the same.'

'No, nothing will ever be the same.' For a moment they just stood there and as he looked down into her lovely face he knew she was right: his life had been altered immeasurably and for ever, simply by loving her. She'd washed the anger out of his heart. He'd stopped looking backwards.

'I feel as if some great weight has been lifted from my shoulders. The past has gone and the future is a bright new page waiting for us to write on it.' Then she turned away quickly, as if she'd given away more of her feelings than she'd meant to show, and started walking down the stairs. 'Can we talk about my proposal soon?' she said. 'I've got so many plans—'

'Proposal?' What proposal? Hadn't she said something about that last night, before she'd stopped talking and started acting? The recollection generated a grin that would have lit up a fair-sized town. Then, 'What plans?'

She glanced up at him, as if to speak, then as they reached the half-landing, she stopped abruptly, seeing the main entrance hall laid out below them. The linen-fold panelling, black and white marble chequered floor, an open fire laid with logs in case the weather turned cold. 'Did we come through here last night?'

'You didn't notice?' he asked, teasing her, but she wasn't paying attention.

'This is so...so...'

'Impossible to heat?' he offered. 'A ridiculous extravagance for one man? A total anachronism in this day and age?'

'So incredibly beautiful. Untouched.'

'It was certainly that way when my grandfather bought it. The house had been in the same family for over four hundred years, and the only concession to the second Elizabethan age was electricity and a single bathroom.'

As she descended to the ground floor she ran her hand over panelling hand-cut by a craftsman centuries before, feeling for the marks of his chisel. 'How could anyone bear to part with this?'

'You can part with anything if the incentive is great enough.'

She turned and looked back up at him, frowning. 'There speaks the hard-headed businessman.'

'Not in this instance.' He followed her down, took her hand, stopping her. 'What proposal, India? What...?' The words died on his lips as a movement behind her caught his attention, and he looked over her head and straight into the eyes of Peter Claibourne.

'Haven't you heard from your lawyers?' she asked. 'I faxed my proposal to my lot yesterday—' She suddenly realised that he wasn't paying attention, that he was more interested in something behind her, and she turned.

'Daddy!' India hadn't called him that in years, but seeing him there made her realise just how worried she'd been. How pleased she was to see him. She crossed to him, gave him a hug. 'Have you any idea how worried I've been? What on earth were you doing in Pakistan?'

'I'm sorry. I didn't think it would take so long to find Kitty, and after that we had to go south—'

'Kitty?' she said. 'Kitty Farraday?' He half turned, so that she could see into the room behind. Standing beside the desk of a book-lined study was a tall, elegant woman who had to be in her mid-fifties but looked younger, despite the silver wings that threw her dark hair into striking contrast. And then she glanced back at Jordan.

His jaw tightened momentarily, then, catching her hand, he crossed to his mother, taking her with him, and bent to kiss her cheek. 'Hello, Kitty,' he said. 'I wasn't expecting you.'

'So I can see. We called at your office first. And the store.' She indicated a pile of press cuttings on the desk beside her. 'Then, reading between the lines…' India was grateful that she left exactly what she'd read between them to their imagination.

'Kitty, may I introduce India Claibourne?'

'Miss Claibourne—'

India stepped forward, offered her hand. 'India, please, Ms Farraday. I understand we have a lot in common.'

'A misplaced passion for a department store,' she agreed. 'And the same fatal attraction for the wrong man.'

India swallowed. Two minutes ago her world had been near perfect. She had given away an empire and gained something greater, finer… 'Wrong man?' she said.

'For pity's sake, Kitty—' Jordan began.

'Enough!' She turned on him, holding up the sheaf of cuttings. 'I haven't seen a newspaper for months, but Christine showed me these.' Jordan's grip on her hand tightened. 'Niall, Bram, and now you. What did you think you were doing, Jordan?'

'Setting up a marriage bureau?' Peter Claibourne offered. Jordan turned and glared at him.

Kitty said, 'Don't be flippant, Peter.' Then she turned on Jordan. 'Well?'

'You know what I was doing.'

'I'm afraid I do. I had to surrender Claibourne & Farraday—'

'*He* took it from you. You begged him. I saw you…'

India turned to her father; his face was impassive.

'He stayed all night and he still took everything. Broke your heart, caused your breakdown…'

'Even if that were true, and it's not, do you think it gives you the right to take your revenge on Peter's daughter?'

India heard the words but for a moment they didn't register. She had to run it through her head on a loop, over and over, until the truth suddenly hit her like an express train, pushing the air out of her, leaving her gasping… Only his hand, fast about hers, preventing her from falling.

She had asked the question. Why hadn't he walked in the day her father had retired and taken over? Now she knew the true answer. He wanted revenge for something that her father had done thirty years ago, when Jordan was just a little boy. Something he'd seen or heard. He wanted to make her beg, just as his mother had begged…

And how he'd made her beg last night…

She swallowed hard as she thought of the night they'd spent together. A night in which they'd given…no, *she'd* given everything. And he'd taken. With nothing in his heart but a desire to hurt her.

'India…' She snatched her hand away. His silence had gone on for too long. 'Please…listen to me.' She took a step back and he turned on his mother. 'Kitty, go away—and take him with you. This is between India and me.'

'No, wait. Stay,' India insisted. No more secrets. No more lies. She had to know everything, no matter what the pain, and, turning to her father, she said, 'What did you do? Tell me what you did to make him hate you so much.'

'I'm sorry, sweetheart. It's not my place to tell anyone what happened between us that night.' He looked at Kitty.

'Nothing happened, India,' she said gently. 'Not because I didn't want it to. But because Peter Claibourne is a gentleman.' Jordan opened his mouth, about to interrupt, but was silenced by a sharp look from his mother. 'My breakdown had nothing to do with your father. It took him to recognise it, though. To see through the brittle shell and realise that I was falling apart inside. I'd been living a lie for a long time. Pretending I hadn't ever loved Jordan's father. Pretending that I'd been happy to see the back of him.'

India sat down as her legs suddenly gave way. 'That's why you gave him his name.'

She smiled a little wryly at that. 'Not all of it. I didn't want anyone to know how much I was hurting…' Above her, Jordan's face was white. 'I was acting out this role, you see. I was the modern career woman who needed no one. Fooling everyone that I was happy with my career. Pretending that I could cope. I should have been an actress. I thought if I could keep the store everything would be all right. I thought if I could seduce Peter he'd have to give it to me, because he was always the sweetest of men. So I rang him and asked him to come and see me. Threw myself at him. All to no purpose. He was coming to see me anyway.'

'And he stayed the night. I saw you together—' Jordan said.

'I'm sorry. I didn't know that. I had no idea...' Kitty took a deep breath. 'He came to give me a letter he'd found. It seems there was never a golden share agreement. It always did seem odd to me, to be honest. One of them would have lost out, and who in their right mind would have signed such a thing when it disinherited his own? The truth is that the agreement was a forgery, cooked up by Charles Claibourne's son and a crooked lawyer to keep William Farraday's young son from taking control.'

'He told you that and you believed it?'

'Peter found a letter written by Charles Junior admitting as much in his father's safe—not exactly something to be proud of, but kept as a kind of insurance policy against the time it might become necessary to break the chain of succession.' She glanced at Jordan. 'If, for example, someone decided to sell the store without consulting the entire partnership.'

India stared at her father. 'Why didn't you tell me? Why did you just go away?'

'I didn't know if the letter still existed. I had to find Kitty. Believe me, it wasn't easy.'

'If I'd been here, if I'd known that your father had been forced to retire, I would have sent it to the lawyers.'

Jordan stirred. 'Why *did* he give it to you? If it wasn't to ease his own conscience?'

She glanced at Peter. 'Do you want to tell them?'

'I wanted Kitty to keep the store. I'd like to say it was because I was noble and good and I knew how much it meant to her. The truth is that Pamela was unhappy. She hadn't bonded with her baby—' he looked at India '—with you. She was suffering, I suppose, from a kind of postnatal depression, and all she wanted to do was go home to India. With me or without me. Then I found the letter in my father's papers and I thought I'd found a lifeline, but as soon as I saw Kitty I knew it was never going to happen. She was saying all the right things, but I could see she was on the edge and about to fall over. I stayed all night, talking to her, hoping against hope that I was wrong.' He shrugged. 'In the morning I called one of her sisters, stayed with her until the doctor arrived, and went back to London.'

'And let my mother go.'

'Something I've never ceased to regret, believe me.'

'Why did she leave me?' India, in those few words, betrayed all the want, the need she'd bottled up in her heart.

'At the time I assumed it was because she wanted nothing to do with any of us. No reminders. I know now that I was wrong about that. My mother tried to bribe her to leave you. And when that didn't work she threatened her. Told her she was unstable, that she'd have her sectioned… The poor frightened child had gone by the time I got back from Kitty's.'

India heard the words. Heard more than they said. 'You've seen her,' she said. 'That's where you've been.'

'Kitty helped me find her. That's why we've been so long. She's in London, Indie. She wants to see you. If you can forgive her. Forgive both of us.'

India could scarcely catch her breath. Her entire life seemed to be turning before her eyes, like a revolving door.

Jordan reached out, took his mother's hand, for a moment unable to speak. Then he turned to Peter Claibourne. 'I'm sorry. I'm so sorry.' The words were simple but heartfelt.

He nodded, but said, 'I don't think I'm the one you should be apologising to.' Then, turning to Kitty, 'I think we've done everything we came to do. Can I give you a lift back to London?'

Kitty picked up a large envelope that was lying on the desk and put it into India's hands. 'I'm passing this on to you. I'm trusting you to make the right choice for the store,' she said, before following Peter out of the room.

The right thing? What was that?

'I was going to tell you,' Jordan said, after a silence that seemed to last for ever.

India stirred. 'Of course you were. Why would you have gone to so much trouble if I was never to discover what you'd done and why? You didn't just want the store. You could have had that any time.'

'I'm not going to lie to you. I'd lived with what I thought was my mother's pain for thirty years. I had no way to hurt your father directly. I thought I could hurt him through you. That he'd know...' He dragged his hands over his face. 'How can I make you believe I wasn't going to go through with it? That two nights ago I looked into a void when I contemplated life without you.'

'That's what you say now,' she said, getting to her feet. Her legs were not entirely trustworthy, but it was time to go.

'I should have made you listen to me last night.'

'Don't blame yourself. I did all the work. Made it easy for you. Surrendered the store, surrendered everything. Lock, stock and barrel,' she said.

She headed towards the door. She wanted to weep for her lost hopes, lost dreams. She tossed the envelope that Kitty Farraday had given her on the desk as she passed. Regaining a department store couldn't begin to make up for everything else she'd lost. There was more to life than shopping.

And in London her mother was waiting for her.

'Goodbye, Jordan.'

He couldn't believe it was happening. Half an hour ago he'd been a man with his whole life in front of him. Made new by the loving touch of a woman who had reached down into his heart, his soul. Changed him beyond recognition.

'Don't go,' he begged. 'Please.'

She stopped with her hand on the doorhandle, but didn't look back. 'How can you ask that?' She turned, pushing her hair behind her ear.

The gesture, so familiar, filled him with sudden hope, and he swiftly crossed to her. 'I can ask it because I love you. Because you have changed me, altered my perceptions, opened my eyes to what is truly important. Everything I said last night—' She flinched at that, and he wanted to fling himself on his knees, plead for her forgiveness. 'Trust me, India. Everything I said, everything I did last night was true. You've bewitched me, redeemed me—'

India wanted to believe that with all her heart. Last

night she'd believed it. Now the words meant nothing… 'I have to go—'

'No!' He slammed his hand against the door as she turned the handle, stopping her from opening it. 'I won't let you leave like this. Do you remember last night how you asked me if I could feel it? I didn't ask you what you were feeling. I knew because I was feeling it with every fibre of my being. Passion, desire.' He took her hand. 'I've shown you the passion, the desire I have for you. Now I'm asking you… Can *you* feel it?' India did not resist as he placed her hand against his heart. 'Can you feel how much I love you, Indie?'

Jordan's heart beat against her palm, strong and powerful, and she was sure that he believed what he was saying. He would say anything, do anything, to get what he wanted. He was a man used to winning and suddenly his prize was walking away.

She took her hand away, reached up and touched her knuckles to his cheek. 'You've won, Jordan. I ceded the store to you yesterday. I wanted to take the store out of our relationship. So you see the letter changes nothing. Be content.'

'Won? You think this is winning? From where I'm standing I'm the world's biggest loser. What can I do? What can I do to make you stay?' He looked baffled, lost. 'Just tell me…'

His heart. That was all she wanted. But she couldn't, wouldn't ask for that. It had to be given freely, as she'd given up her claim to the store, no strings attached. And the moment for that was past.

'What will you do?' he asked.

'Afterwards?' she asked. It was the question she'd asked him about his mother. And Kitty Farraday was a fine example of a woman who had remade her life. Made some good out of it. 'I'm going to see my mother, Jordan.' She tried a wry smile. It felt as if her face was breaking. 'But first I'd better go home and get dressed in something other than last night's finery.'

'I'll take you.'

'No!' Then, 'If you'll phone for a car—'

'No, Indie. I'm taking you home. I'm not leaving your side until you're prepared to listen to me. However long it takes.' And he stepped back, allowed her to open the door.

She picked up her dress, still hooked over the banister with his jacket, where they'd abandoned them last night, before turning to face him. 'You're forgetting something, Jordan. You don't have time for such nonsense. You have a department store to run.'

'No!' Then, 'No, wait!' he shouted. She slung the slender red silk gown over her shoulder and forced herself to keep going. 'My jacket. Look in my jacket pocket. Inside. You'll find an envelope. It's got your name on it.'

With a sigh, she turned, picked up the jacket, looked in his inside pocket. 'No envelope, Jordan.'

'It's there. I put it there last night…' He took the jacket from her, searched all the pockets. 'It must have fallen out. Come on.' And he seized her hand, refusing to listen to her objections as he flung open the French windows that led onto the lawn.

The grass was damp, her feet were soaked, and she was almost running to keep up with his long strides, bumping into him as he stopped without warning. 'There,' he said. 'That's it.' On the path in front of her lay a square cream envelope, her name slightly fuzzy where the ink had run, but still clear. 'Thank God,' he said.

'Jordan? What is it?'

'It's for you. Pick it up.' She bent and picked it up offered it to him, but he held up his hands, distancing himself from it. 'I want you to open it. I want you to read it.'

Inside were two sheets of papers. One was a copy of a letter, dated the previous day, to his solicitor, renouncing any claim to control of Claibourne & Farraday.

The other was handwritten. There were only two words.

'I surrender.' Just two words. Beneath them he'd signed his name in full.

India read them again, then looked up. 'I don't understand.'

He remained an arm's length distance from her. 'What exactly don't you understand? I—that's me—Jordan David Farraday—surrender. As in capitulate, deliver up yield, relinquish, renounce.' He sank to his knees on the soft grass. 'I am on my knees surrendering to you, Indie.

Last night. 'This was in your pocket last night.. before...?' It was his heart. Freely given. No strings attached.

'I was going to put that in your hand last night, Indie Tell you everything before you opened it so that you'd know that, whatever I did, I had no motive other than love. It was that incentive thing... My incentive to surrender outweighed a million times my desire for revenge I made the belated discovery that sometimes losing can make a man a winner.' He took both her hands in his crushing the damp paper. 'You are the only prize I want.'

India was smiling...grinning from ear to ear...unable to stop. 'This...um...surrender. Was it just Claibourne & Farraday you were surrendering?'

His face was grave. 'You've already got everything

else. I gave you my heart. My spirit.' The sexy precursor to his smile appeared at the corner of his mouth. 'You helped yourself to my body.'

'Then we're finally, truly, equal partners?'

'Equal in everything.'

And she, too, sank to her knees. 'Then the proposal I sent to the lawyers, about using my name to open my own store—'

'Is rejected. Out of hand. The names go together. Yours and mine. Eternally. I've got a proposal of my own, India Claibourne, and there's only one answer I'm prepared to contemplate.' She waited for him to go on, but he said nothing. Though there was a smile hovering just beneath the surface, waiting to break out.

'Yes?' she prompted.

'That's the answer I was looking for,' he said. And the letters she was holding slipped from her fingers and fluttered away on the morning breeze as he took her in his arms to seal their merger with a kiss.

EPILOGUE

CITY DIARY, *London Evening Post*

WE'VE had a lot of fun following the flurry of romances between the Claibournes and Farradays in this column during the last few months, but we're delighted to send Jordan Farraday and his lovely bride-to-be India Claibourne our warmest congratulations and good wishes today, on the occasion of their wedding.

Our best wishes also go to Niall and Romana Macaulay and Bram and Flora Gifford, whose recent marriages are to be blessed at the same time in a joint ceremony cementing the ties between these two great families.

This is a bright new era for Claibourne & Farraday. With the new generation now partners in every sense, the uncertainties of recent months are a thing of the past and London's most stylish store can only go from strength to strength.

Jordan turned as, at a signal from the door, the organist stopped improvising and launched into the 'Entry of the Queen of Sheba'. Niall came first, with Romana wearing a high-waisted dress with a red and gold bodice over a softly draped skirt that hid the early evidence of approaching motherhood.

Niall looked about ten feet tall, he thought, as his cousin looked at his wife protectively, adoringly.

Come on, he urged impatiently. Come on.

Bram entered next, with Flora. She was wearing a simple tailored mandarin jacket in silver and blue, with a long blue silk skirt, her hair piled up loosely so that soft tendrils fell about her cheeks. Bram grinned at Jordan as he and Flora took their places. To see his cousins so happy was a joy in itself.

Then a hush fell, the music changed from Handel to Wagner, the classic bridal entry, and he turned and saw India. A shaft of light behind her left her in silhouette as she paused, glanced back for a moment to ensure that her posse of tiny bridesmaids was ready. Happy, she turned to her father and placed her hand on his arm, before leaning towards him and tucking her veil to one side in order to kiss his cheek.

That done, she looked ahead to where he was waiting and began to move towards him. A vision in gold and white. His life, his heart, his love.

With every step of her long walk down the broad aisle of the church her gaze remained fixed upon his face. She drew level with him, handed her flowers to someone and then, as he reached out his hand to her, placed her own in his. He took it, held it. And with his eyes he silently vowed to her, as he soon would before God and the congregation, that, having won her against all odds, he would never let her go. That he would honour her, love and cherish her, for the rest of his life.

As if she could read his thoughts, she gently squeezed his fingers before she turned to face the clergyman.

'Dearly beloved...'

Afterwards, outside in the milling crowd, India went straight to her mother and hugged her. 'I'm so glad you're here,' she said. There had been tears at their meeting. Long and, for both of them, sometimes painful explanations. A lifetime of memories and regret.

'You can't begin to know how glad I am that I came.' Pamela Claibourne looked to where her ex-husband was chatting to his new son-in-law. 'How happy I am that Peter found me again.'

It was enough. Today the past was forever put behind them. There was only the future.

She paused briefly with Jordan, posing with her sisters and their new husbands outside the lych-gate of the church while a curious press took photographs, before they walked back hand-in-hand through the garden. 'I see the gold,' Jordan murmured, leaning close to murmur in her ear. 'What happened to the burgundy?'

India looked up at him, making no attempt to hide her smile as she extended her left hand, where her ruby and diamond engagement ring nestled against her new wedding ring. 'This is enough for public display, don't you think? We aren't running a PR exercise here.'

'True. Even so, I didn't think you'd be able to resist just a touch—'

She grinned. 'Did I say I'd resisted? You wouldn't want me to be too obvious, would you? Or maybe you'd like me to lift my skirt and show off my garter?' And, leaving her new husband to catch his breath as they reached the marquee set out on the riverside lawns, she took her place in the receiving line to greet their guests.

CELEBRITY magazine

We're delighted to bring our readers stunning photographs of the recent wedding of India Claibourne and

Jordan Farraday, partners in our favourite department store. The presence of her mother, after many years' estrangement, clearly brought special joy to India.

Peter Claibourne, the bride's father, whose recent heart attack caused such concern to his family, was looking fit and well, and rarely left his former wife's side. Friends say that the two, who met again recently when Peter was convalescing, have become very close.

The bride's half-sisters, Romana and Flora, seen here with their new husbands, chose this wonderful occasion to have their own marriages blessed.

Their stunning gowns, while individual in style, each had an exquisite bodice in a difference colour, made from a stunning new fabric discovered by Flora during a visit to the beautiful island of Saraminda.

Jordan and India have left for a leisurely honeymoon in the United States before India takes her place at the head of the new board of Claibourne & Farraday.

We wish them all well in their new lives.